Rebecca Mary

Annie Hamilton Donnell

Rebecca Mary

Annie Hamilton Donnell

© 1st World Library – Literary Society, 2004
PO Box 2211
Fairfield, IA 52556
www.1stworldlibrary.org
First Edition

LCCN: 2004091161

Softcover ISBN: 1-59540-607-7
eBook ISBN: 1-59540-707-3

Purchase *"Rebecca Mary"*
as a traditional bound book at:
www.1stWorldLibrary.org/purchase.asp?ISBN=1-59540-607-7

1st World Library Literary Society is a nonprofit
organization dedicated to promoting literacy by:

- Creating a free internet library accessible from any
  computer worldwide.
- Hosting writing competitions and offering book
  publishing scholarships.

Readers interested in supporting literacy
through sponsorship, donations or
membership please contact:
literacy@1stworldlibrary.org
Check us out at: www.1stworldlibrary.org

Contents

The Hundred and Oneth

Rebecca Mary took another stitch. Then another. "Ninety-sevvun, ninety-eight," she counted aloud, her little pointed face gravely intent. She waited the briefest possible space before she took ninety-nine. It was getting very close to the Time now. "At the hundred an' oneth," Rebecca Mary whispered. "It's almost it." Her breath came quicker under her tight little dress. Between her thin, light eyebrows a crease deepened anxiously.

"Ninety - n-i-n-e," she counted, "one hun-der-ed" - it was so very close now! The next stitch would be the hundred and oneth. Rebecca Mary's face suddenly grew quite white.

"I'll wait a m-minute," she decided; "I'm just a little scared. When you've been lookin' head to the hundred and oneth so LONG and you get the very next door to it, it scares you a little. I'll wait until - oh, until Thomas Jefferson crows, before I sew the hundred and oneth."

Thomas Jefferson was prospecting under the currant bushes. Rebecca Mary could see him distinctly, even with her nearsighted little eyes, for Thomas Jefferson was snow-white. Once in a while he stalked dignifiedly out of the bushes and crowed. He might do it again any minute now.

The great sheet billowed and floated round Rebecca Mary, scarcely whiter than her face. She held her needle poised, waiting the signal of Thomas Jefferson. At any ***[min - ?]*** min He was coming out now! A fleck of snow-white was pricking the green of the currant leaves.

"He's out. Any minute he'll begin to cr - " He was already beginning! The warning signals were out - chest expanding, neck elongating, and great white wing aflap.

"I'm just a little scared," breathed the child in the foam of the sheet. Then Thomas Jefferson crowed.

"Hundred and one!" Rebecca Mary cried out, clearly, courage born within her at the crucial instant. The Time - the Time - had come. She had taken her last stitch.

"It's over," she panted. "It always was a-coming, and it's come. I knew it would. When it's come, you don't feel quite so scared. I'm glad it's over."

She folded up the great sheet carefully, making all the edges meet with painful precision. It took time. She had left the needle sticking in the unfinished seam - in the hundred-and-oneth stitch - and close beside it was a tiny dot of red to "keep the place."

"Rebecca! Rebecca Mary!" Aunt Olivia always called like that. If there had been still another name - Rebecca Mary Something Else - she would have called: "Rebecca! Rebecca Mary! Rebecca Mary Something Else!"

Annie Hamilton Donnell

"Yes'm; I'm here."

"Where's 'here'?" sharply.

"HERE - the grape-arbor, I mean."

"Have you got your sheet?"

"I - yes'm."

"Is your stent 'most done?"

Rebecca Mary rose slowly to her reluctant little feet, and with the heavy sheet across her arm went to meet the sharp voice. At last the Time had come.

"Well?" Aunt Olivia was waiting for her answer. Rebecca Mary groaned. Aunt Olivia would not think it was "well."

"Well, Rebecca Mary Plummer, you came to fetch my answer, did you? You got your stent 'most done?" Aunt Olivia's hands were extended for the folded sheet.

"I've got it DONE, Aunt 'Livia," answered little Rebecca Mary, steadily. Her slender figure, in its quaint, scant dress, looked braced as if to meet a shock. But Rebecca Mary was terribly afraid.

"Every mite o' that seam? Then I guess you can't have done it very well; that's what I guess! If it ain't done well, you'll have to take it - "

"Wait - please, won't you wait, Aunt 'Livia? I've got to say something. I mean, I've got all the over-'n'-overing I'm ever going to do done. THAT'S what's done. The hundred-and-oneth stitch was my stent, and it's done. I'm not ever going to take the hundred and twoth. I've decided."

Understanding filtered drop by drop into Aunt Olivia's bewildered brain. She gasped at the final drop.

"Not ever going to take another stitch?" she repeated, with a calmness that was awfuler than storm.

"No'm."

"You've decided?"

"Yes'm."

"May I ask when this - this state of mind began?"

Rebecca Mary girded herself afresh. She had such need of recruiting strength.

"It's been coming on," she said. "I've felt it. I knew all the time it was a-coming - and then it came."

It seemed to be all there. Why must she say any more? But still Aunt Olivia waited, and Rebecca Mary read grim displeasure in capitals across the gray field of her face. The little figure stiffened more and more.

"I've over-'n'-overed 'leven sheets," the steady little voice went on, because Aunt Olivia was waiting, and it must, "and you said I did 'em pretty well. I tried to. I was going to do the other one well, till you said there was going to be another dozen. I couldn't BEAR another dozen, Aunt Olivia, so I decided to stop. When

Thomas Jefferson crowed I sewed the hundred-and-oneth stitch. That's all there's ever a-going to be."

Rebecca Mary stepped back a step or two, as if finishing a speech and retiring from her audience. There was even the effect of a bow in the sudden collapse of the stiff little body. It was Aunt Olivia's turn now to respond - and Aunt Olivia responded:

"You've had your say; now I'll have mine. Listen to me, Rebecca Mary Plummer! Here's this sheet, and here's this needle in it. When you get good and ready you can go on sewing. You won't have anything to eat till you do. I've got through."

The grim figure swept right-about face and tramped into the house as though to the battle-roll of drums. Rebecca Mary stayed behind, face to face with her fate.

"She's a Plummer, so it'll be SO," Rebecca Mary thought, with the dull little thud of a weight falling into her heart. Rebecca Mary was a Plummer too, but she did not think of that, unless the un-swerving determination in her stout little heart was the unconscious recognition of it.

"I wonder" - her gaze wandered out towards the currant-bushes and came to rest absently on Thomas Jefferson's big, white bulk - "I wonder if it hurts very much." She meant, to starve. A long vista of food-less days opened before her, and in their contemplation the weight in her heart grew very heavy indeed.

"We were GOING to have layer-cake for supper. I'm VERY fond of layer-cake," Rebecca Mary sighed, "I suppose, though, after a few weeks" - she shuddered - "I shall be glad to have ANYTHING - just common things, like crackers and skim-milk. Perhaps I shall want to eat a - horse. I've heard of folks - You get very unparticular when you're starving."

It was five o'clock. They WERE going to have supper at half past. She could hear the tea things clinking in the house. She stole up to a window. There was Aunt Olivia setting the layer-cake on the table. It looked plump and rich, and it was sugared on top.

"There's strawberry jam in between it," mused Rebecca Mary, regretfully. "I wish it was apple jelly. I could bear it better if it was apple jelly." But it was jam. And there was honey, too, to eat with Aunt Olivia's little fluffy biscuits. How very fond Rebecca Mary was of honey!

Aunt Olivia stood in the kitchen doorway and rang the supper bell in long, steady clangs just as usual. But no one responded just as usual, and by the token she knew Rebecca Mary had not taken the other stitch that lay between her and supper.

"She's a Plummer," sighed Aunt Olivia, inwardly, unrealizing her own Plummership, as little Rebecca Mary had unrealized hers. Each recognized only the other's. The pity that both must be Plummers!

Rebecca Mary stayed out of doors until bedtime. She made but one confidant.

"I've done it, Thomas Jefferson," she said, sadly. "You ought to be sorry for me, because if you hadn't crowed I shouldn't have sewed the hundred and oneth. But

Annie Hamilton Donnell

you're not really to BLAME," she added, hastily, mindful of Thomas Jefferson's feelings. "I should have done it sometime if you hadn't crowed. I knew it was coming. I suppose now I shall have to starve. You'd think it was pretty hard to starve, I guess, Thomas Jefferson."

Thomas Jefferson made certain gloomy responses in his throat to the effect that he was always starving; that any contributions on the spot in the way of corn kernels, wheat grains, angleworms - any little delicacies of the kind - would be welcome. And Rebecca Mary, understanding, led the way to the corn bin. In the dark hours that followed, the intimacy between the great white rooster and the little white girl took on tenderer tones.

At breakfast next morning - at dinner time - at supper - Rebecca Mary absented herself from the house. Aunt Olivia set on the meals regularly and waited with tightening heartstrings. It did not seem to occur to her to eat her own portions. She tasted no morsel of all the dainties she got together wistfully. At nightfall the second day she began to feel real alarm. She put on her bonnet and went to the minister's. He was rather a new minister, and the Plummers had always required a good deal of time to make acquaintance. But in the present stress of her need Aunt Olivia did not stop to think of that.

"You must come over and - and do something," she said, at the conclusion of her strange little story. "It seems to me it's time for the minister to step in."

"What can I do, Miss Plummer?" the embarrassed young man ejaculated, with a feeling of helplessness.

"Talk to her," groaned Aunt Olivia, in her agony. "Tell her what her duty is. Rebecca Mary might listen to the minister. All she's got to do is to take just one stitch to show her submission. It won't take but an instant. I've got supper all out on the kitchen table - I don't care if it's ten o'clock at night!"

"It isn't a case for the minister. It's a case for the Society for the Prevention of Cruelty to Children!" fumed the minister's kind little wife inwardly. And she stole away in the twilight to deal with little Rebecca Mary herself. She came back to the minister by and by, red-eyed and fierce.

"You needn't go over; I've been. It won't do any good, Robert. That poor, stiff-willed, set little thing is starving by inches!"

"I think her aunt is, too!"

"Well, perhaps - I can't help it, Robert, perhaps the - aunt - ought - to."

"My dear! - Felicia!"

"I told you I couldn't help it. She is so hungry, Robert! If you had seen her - What do you think she was doing when I got there?"

"Crying?"

"Crying! She was laughing. *I* cried. She sat there under some grapevines watching a great white rooster eat his supper. His name, I think, is Thomas Jefferson."

"Yes, Thomas Jefferson," agreed the minister, with the

Annie Hamilton Donnell

assurance of acquaintance. For Thomas Jefferson was one of his parishioners.

"Well, she was laughing at him in the shakiest, hungriest little voice you ever heard. 'Is it good?' she says. 'It LOOKS good.' He was eating raw corn. 'If I could, I'd eat supper with you when you're VERY hungry, you don't mind eating things raw.' Then she saw me."

"Well?"

"Well, I coaxed her, Robert. It didn't do any good. Tomorrow somebody must go there and interfere."

"She must be a remarkably strange child," the minister mused. He was thinking of the holding-out powers of the three children he had a half-ownership in.

"I don't think Rebecca Mary IS a child, Robert. She must be fifty years old, at the least. She and her aunt are about the same age. Perhaps if her mother had lived, or she hadn't made so many sheets, or learned to knit and darn and cook - " The minister's kind little wife finished out her sentence with a sigh. She took up a little garment in dire straits to be mended. It suggested things to the minister.

"Can Rhoda darn?"

"RHODA!"

"Or make sheets and bread and things?"

"Robert, don't you feel well? Where is the pain?" But the laugh in the pleasant blue eyes died out suddenly.

Little Rebecca Mary lay too heavy on the minister's wife's heart for mirth.

Aunt Olivia went into Rebecca Mary's room in the middle of the night. She had been in three times before.

"She looks thinner than she did last time," Aunt Olivia murmured, distressedly. "Tomorrow night - how long do children live without eating? It's four meals now - four meals is a great many for a little thin thing to go without!" Aunt Olivia had been without four meals too; she would have been able to judge how it felt - if she had remembered that part. She stood in her scant, long nightgown, gazing down at the little sleeper. The veil was down and her heart was in her eyes.

Rebecca Mary threw out her arm and sighed. "It LOOKS good, Thomas Jefferson," she murmured. "When you're VERY hungry you can eat things raw." Suddenly the child sat up in bed, wide-eyed and wild. She did not seem to see Aunt Olivia at all.

"Once I ate a pie!" she cried. "It wasn't a whole one, but I should eat a whole one now - I think I should eat the PLATE now." She swayed back and forth weakly, awake and not awake.

"Once I ate a layer-cake. There was jam in it. I wouldn't care if it was apple jelly in it now - I'd LIKE apple jelly in it now. Once I ate a pudding and a doughnut a-n-d - a - a - I think it was a horse. I'd eat a horse now. Hush! Don't tell Aunt Olivia, but I'm going to eat - to - e-at - Thom-as - Jeffer - " She swayed back on the pillows again. Aunt Olivia shook her in an agony of fear - she was so white - she lay so still.

Annie Hamilton Donnell

"Rebecca! Rebecca Mary! Rebecca Mary PLUMMER!" Aunt Olivia shrilled in her ear. "You get right out o' bed this minute and come downstairs and eat your supper! It's high time you had something in your stomach - I don't care if it's twelve o'clock. You get right out o' bed REBECCA MARY!"

Aunt Olivia had the limp little figure in her arms, shaking it gently again and again. Rebecca's startled eyes flew open. In that instant was born inspiration in the brain of Aunt Olivia. She thought of an appeal to make.

"Do you want ME to starve, too? Right here before your face and eyes? I haven't eat a mouthful since you did, and I shan't till you DO."

Rebecca Mary slid to the floor with a soft thud of little brown, bare feet. Slow comprehension dawned in her eyes. "Are***[-]*** did you say YOU was starving, too?"

"Yes" - grimly.

"Does it hurt you - too?"

"Yes" - unsteadily.

"VERY much?"

"YES."

"Why don't you eat something?"

"Because you don't. I'm waiting for you to."

"Shan't you ever?"

"Not if you don't."

Rebecca Mary caught her breath in a sob. "Shall I be - to blame?" She was moving towards the door now. With an irresistible impulse Aunt Olivia gathered her in her arms, and covered her lean little face with kisses.

"You poor little thing! You poor little thing! You poor little thing!" over and over.

Rebecca Mary gazed up into the softened face and read something there. It took her breath away. She could not believe it without further proof.

"You don't - I don't suppose you LOVE me?" panted Rebecca Mary. But Aunt Olivia was gone out of the room in a swirl of white nightgown.

"Everything's on the table," she called back from the stairs. "I'm going to light a fire. You come right down. I think it's high time - " her voice trailing out thinly.

"She does," murmured Rebecca Mary, radiant of face.

At half past twelve o'clock they both ate supper, both in their scant, white nightgowns, both very hungry indeed. But before she sat down in her old place at the table, Rebecca Mary went round to Aunt Olivia's place and whispered something rather shyly in her ear. She had been by herself in a corner of the room for a moment.

"I've sewed the hundred and twoth," Rebecca Mary whispered.

The Thousand Quilt

"Good afternoon," Rebecca Mary said, politely.

The minister's wife was cutting little trousers out of big ones - the minister's big ones. It was the old puzzle of how to steer clear of the thin places.

"Boys grow so!" sighed, tenderly, the minister's wife, over her work. She had not heard the voice from the doorway.

"Good afternoon" - again.

It was a quaint little figure in tight red calico standing there. It might easily have stepped down from some old picture on the wall. Rebecca Mary had a bundle in her arms. It was so large that it obscured breast and face, and only a pair of grave blue eyes, presided over by thin, light brows, seemed visible to the minister's wife. The trousers puzzle merged into this one. Now who could -

"Oh! Oh, it's Miss Plummer's little girl Rebecca," she said, cordially.

"Rebecca Mary her NIECE," came, a little muffled, from behind the great bundle.

Annie Hamilton Donnell

"Rebecca Mary's nie*** - *** Oh, you mean Miss Plummer's niece, and your whole name is that! But I suppose she calls you Rebecca or Becky, for short? Walk in, Rebecca."

But Rebecca Mary was struggling with the paralyzing vision of Aunt Olivia calling her Becky. She had passed by the lesser wonder of being called Rebecca without the Mary.

"Oh no'm, indeed; Aunt 'Livia never shortens me," gently gasped the child. And the minister's wife, measuring from the bundle down, smiled to herself. There did not seem much room for shortening.

"But walk in, dear - you're going to walk in? I hope you have come to make me a little call?"

Rebecca Mary struggled out of her paralysis. Here was occasion for new embarrassment. For Rebecca Mary was honest.

"N-o'm I mean, not a LITTLE call. I've come to spend the afternoon," she said, slowly, "and I've brought my work."

The bundle - the great bundle - was her work! She advanced into the room and began carefully to unroll it. It was the turn of the minister's wife to be paralyzed. She pushed forward a chair, and the child sat down in it.

"It's my Thousand Quilt that I'm making for Aunt 'Livia," explained Rebecca Mary. "It's 'most done. There's a thousand pieces in it, and I'm on the nine hundred and ninety-oneth. I thought proberly you'd have some work, so I brought mine."

"Yes, I see - " The minister's wife stood looking down at the tight little red figure among the gorgeous waves of the Thousand Quilt. They eddied and surged around it in dizzy reds and purples and greens. She was conscious of being a little seasick, and for relief she turned back to the puzzle of the little trousers. It had been in her mind at first to express sorrow at Rhoda's being unfortunately away - and the boys. Now she was glad she hadn't, for it was quite plain enough that the visitor had not come to spend the afternoon with the minister's children, but with the minister's wife.

"It isn't she that's young - it's I," thought the minister's wife, with kind, laughing eyes. "She's old enough to be my mother." "How old are you, dear?" she added, aloud.

"Me? I guess you mean Aunt 'Livia, don't you? It's Aunt 'Livia's birthday I'm making it for, it's going to be a present. Once she gave me a present on my birthday."

Once! - the minister's wife remembered Rhoda's birthdays and the boys'. Taken altogether, such a host of little birthdays! But this little old, old visitor seemed to have had but one.

"My birthday is two days quicker than Aunt 'Livia's is," volunteered the visitor, sociably. "We're 'most twins, you see. Aunt 'Livia was fifty-six that time she gave me the present. She's agoing to be fifty-nine when I give her this quilt - it's taken me ever since to make it."

Annie Hamilton Donnell

The minister's wife looked up from her cutting. So Rebecca Mary was only fifty-nine!

"It's quite a long quilt," sighed Rebecca Mary. But pride woke in her eyes as she gazed out on the splendors of the green and purple sea. "A Thousand Quilt has so many stitches in it, but when you sew'em all yourself - when you sew every single stitch - " The pride in Rebecca Mary's grave blue eyes grew and grew.

"Robert," the minister's wife said that night to the minister, "it's an awful quilt, but you ought to have seen her eyes! It's taken her three years to make it - maybe you wouldn't be proud yourself!"

"Maybe YOU wouldn't, if Rhoda had made it."

"RHODA! Robert, she sewed one square of patchwork once and it made her sick. I had to put her to bed. Speaking of 'once' reminds me - once Rebecca Mary had a birthday present, Robert." She waited a little anxiously for him to understand. The minister always understood, but sometimes he made her wait.

"Felicia, are you trying to make me cry?" he said, and she was satisfied. She went across to him, as she always did when she wanted to cry herself. The floor was strewn with the tiniest boy's engine and cars, and she remembered, as she zigzagged among them, that they had been one of his very last birthday presents.

"It was - Robert, what do you think the present was? I'll give you three guesses, but I advise you to guess a rooster."

"Thomas Jefferson," murmured the minister, as one who was acquainted.

"Yes, that is his name. How did you remember? She is very fond of him - he is her intimatest friend, she says. So she is under great obligations to her aunt. It's a large quilt, but it's none too large to 'cover' Thomas Jefferson. I'm going to help her buy a lining and cotton batting."

"Cracked corn will make a good lining, but cotton bat - "

"Robert, this is not a comedy! If you'd seen Rebecca Mary, and the quilt, you'd call it a tragedy. You couldn't surprise me any if you told me she'd quilted it herself!"

Down the road from Aunt Olivia's farm, across its southern boundary fence, romped and shouted all day long the Tony Trumbullses. No one, except possibly their mother, was quite certain how many of them there were; it was a dizzy process to take their census. They were never still, in little brown bare limbs nor shrill voices. From sunup to sundown the Tony Trumbullses raced and laughed. Certainly they were happy.

The minister's wife had not dared to tell her Caller of the afternoon that the minister's children were down there shouting and racing with the little Tony Trumbullses. Dear, no! - not after Rebecca Mary in the course of conversation had said that Aunt Olivia did not countenance the Tony Trumbullses. Rebecca Mary did not say "countenance," but it meant that.

"Her aunt won't let her play with them, Robert. And she'd like to - you needn't tell me Rebecca Mary wouldn't like to! I saw it in her poor little solemn eyes. Besides, she said she asked her aunt once to let her. Robert, aunts are cruel; I never knew it before. They've no business bringing up little Rebecca Marys!"

"My dear! Felicia!" But in the minister's eyes was agreement.

Aunt Olivia took afternoon naps with punctilious regularity - Aunt Olivia herself was punctilious regularity. At half past one, day upon day, she hung out the dish towel, hung up her kitchen apron, and walked with unswerving course into her bedroom. There, disposed upon the dainty bed in rigid lines of unrest, she rested. The naps were often long ones.

A little after the afternoon that Rebecca Mary spent at the minister's the birthday quilt was finished. The thousandth tiny piece was neatly over-'n'-overed to its gorgeous expanse. But Rebecca Mary was not content. She longed to make it complete. She wanted to surprise Aunt 'Livia with it, as Aunt 'Livia on that momentous birthday of her own had surprised her with the little fluff-ball of yellow down that had grown into Thomas Jefferson. That had been such a beautiful surprise, but this - Aunt 'Livia had seen the quilt so many, many times! She had taught Rebecca Mary's stiff little fingers to set the first stitches in it; she had made her rip out this purple square and that pink-checked one, and this one and that one and that. Oh, Aunt 'Livia was ACQUAINTED with the quilt! It would not be much of a surprise.

But Rebecca Mary set her little pointed chin between

her little brown palms and pondered, and out of the pondering grew a plan so ambitious and so daring that Rebecca Mary gasped in the throes of it. But she held her ground and entertained it intrepidly. She even grew on friendly terms with it in the end. Here was a way to surprise Aunt 'Livia; Rebecca Mary would do it! That it would entail an almost endless amount of work did not daunt her: Rebecca Mary was a Plummer, and Plummers were not to be daunted. The long vista of patient hours of trying labor that the plan opened up before her set her blood tingling like a warrior's on the eve of battle. What were long, patient hours to a Plummer? Rebecca Mary girded up her loins and went to meet them.

Thereafter at Aunt Olivia's nap times Rebecca Mary disappeared. Day upon day, week upon week, she stole quietly away when the door of Aunt Olivia's bedroom shut. The first time she went oddly loaded down with what would have appeared - if there had been any one for it to "appear" to be a bundle of long sticks. She made two trips into the unknown that first day. The second time the bundle looked much like that one over which her grave blue eyes had peered at the minister's wife when she went to spend the afternoon with her.

It was spring when the mysterious disappearances began. It was summer before Aunt Olivia woke up - not from her nap, but from her inattention. Quite suddenly she came upon the realization that Rebecca Mary was not about the house; nor about the grounds, for she instituted prompt search. She went to all the child's odd little haunts - the grapery, the orchard, the corn-house, even to her own beloved back yard, full of sweet-scented hiding-nooks dear to a child, but sacred ground to Aunt Olivia. Rebecca Mary sometimes did

Annie Hamilton Donnell

her "stents" there as a special privilege; she might be there now, unprivileged. Aunt Olivia's back yard was almost as full of flowery delights to Rebecca Mary as it was to Aunt Olivia.

The child was not there - not anywhere. Aunt Olivia sought for Thomas Jefferson to inquire of him, but Thomas Jefferson was missing too. She went the rounds again. Where could the child be?

It was a hot, stinging day in late June when Aunt Olivia's suspicions awoke. They had been long in rousing, but, once alert, they developed rapidly into certainties. Her pale eyes glistened, her thin nostrils dilated - Aunt Olivia's whole lean, sharp, unemotional person put on suspicion. The child had gone to see the Tony Trumbullses.

"My land!" ejaculated Aunt Olivia, "after all my forbidding! And she a Plummer!" She sat down suddenly as though a little faint. She had never known a Plummer to disobey before; it was a new experience. It took time to get used to it, and she sat still a long time, rigid and grim, on the edge of the chair. Then as suddenly as she had sat down she got up. It could not be - she refused to entertain the suspicion longer. Rebecca Mary had NOT gone there to that forbidden place; she was in the garden somewhere. Aunt Olivia, a little stiff as if from a chill, went once more in search of the child.

"Rebecca! Rebecca Mary!" she called, at regular intervals. Then sharply, "Rebecca Mary Plummer!" Her voice had thin cadences of suspicion lurking in it against its will.

But there seemed really no doubt. One by one incriminating circumstances occurred to Aunt Olivia. Rebecca Mary had longed to go so much; the Tony Trumbullses, one at a time or in a tumultuous body, had urged her so often; she herself had more than once caught the child gazing wistfully, in passing by, at the bewildering, deafening, frolics of the little Tony Trumbullses. Once Rebecca Mary had asked to go barefoot, as they went. Once she had let out the tight little braids in her neck and rumpled her thin little hair. Once Aunt Olivia had come upon her PLAYING. The remembrance of it now tightened the lines around Aunt Olivia's lips. The child had been running wildly about the yard, shouting in a strange, excited, ridiculous way. When Aunt Olivia in stern displeasure had demanded explanations, she had run on recklessly, calling back over her shoulder: "Don't stop me! I'm a Tony Trumbull!"

"My land!" breathed Aunt Olivia, taking back the suspicion to her breast. "After all my forbidding she's gone down there. She's BEEN going down there dear knows how long. She's waited till I took my naps an' then went. A PLUMMER!"

There was really nowhere else she could have gone. She had never wanted to go anywhere else, except to the minister's, and Rebecca Mary was punctilious and would not think of going THERE again till the minister's wife had returned her visit.

But Aunt Olivia waited. As usual, she went to her room next day at nap time and closed the door behind her. But when a little figure slipped down the road towards the forbidden place a moment later, she was watching behind her blinds. She was groaning as if in pain.

The little figure began to run staidly. Aunt Olivia groaned again. The child was in a hurry to get there - she couldn't wait to walk! There was guilt in every motion of the little figure.

"And she runs like a Plummer," groaned Aunt Olivia.

The next day, and the next, Aunt Olivia watched behind her blinds. The fourth day she put on her afternoon dress and followed the hurrying little figure. Not at once - Aunt Olivia did not hurry. There was a sad reluctance in every movement. It seemed a terrible thing to be following Rebecca Mary - Rebecca Mary Plummer to a forbidden place.

Afar off Aunt Olivia heard faintly the shoutings that always heralded an approach to the Tony Trumbullses, and shuddered. The tumult kept growing clearer; she thought she detected a wild, excited little shout that might be Rebecca Mary's. Her thin lips set into a stern, straight line.

A splash of red caught Aunt Olivia's eye as she drew nearer the joyous whirl of little children. Rebecca Mary wore a little tight red dress. The coil seemed closing in about the child.

Close to the southern boundary fence of Aunt Olivia's land stood an old empty barn. It had been a place for storing surplus hay, once, when there had been surplus hay. For many years now it had been empty. As Aunt Olivia approached it she noticed that its great sliding door was open. Strange, when for so long it had been shut!

"If that old barn door ain't open!" breathed Aunt Olivia, stopping in her astonishment. "I ain't seen it open before in these ten years. Now, what I want to know is, who opened it? Likely as not those screeching little wild Injuns." She strode across the stubby grass-ground to the barn and peered into its cool, dim depths. Then Aunt Olivia uttered a little, bewildered cry. Gradually the dimness took on light and the whole startling picture within unfolded itself to her astonished eyes.

Rebecca Mary was quilting. She was stooping earnestly over a gay expanse of purples and reds and greens. Her little tight red back was towards Aunt Olivia; it looked bent and strained. Rebecca Mary's eyes were very close to the gay expanse.

Suddenly Rebecca Mary began to speak, and Aunt Olivia's widened eyes discovered a great, white rooster pecking about under the quilt. His big, snowy bulk stood out distinct in the shadow of it.

"I'm glad we're 'most through. Aren't you, Thomas Jefferson? It's been a pretty LONG quilt. You get sort of tired when you quilt a LONG quilt. It makes your back creak when you unbend it; and when you quilt in a barn, of course you can't see without squinching, and it hurts your eyes to squinch."

Silence again, except for the industrious peck-peck of the great white rooster. Aunt Olivia stood very still.

"You've been a great help, Thomas Jefferson," began again the voice of Rebecca Mary, after a little. "I'm very much obliged to you, as I've said before. I don't know what I should have done without you. No, you

Annie Hamilton Donnell

needn't answer. I couldn't hear a word you said. You can't hear with cotton in both o' your ears," Rebecca Mary sighed. There was no cotton in Aunt Olivia's ears to shut out the soft little sound. "But of course you have to wear it in, on account o' your conscience. It's conscience cotton, Thomas Jefferson. I've explained before, but I don't know's you understood. It seems a little unpolite to wear it in my ears, with you here keeping me comp'ny. I s'pose you think it's un - unsociable. But Aunt Olivia doesn't allow me to 'sociate with the Tony Trumbullses. Oh, Thomas Jefferson, I wish she'd allow me to 'sociate!"

Aunt Olivia found herself wishing she had conscience cotton in both o' her ears.

"They're such nice, cheerful little children! It makes you want to go right over their fence and hollow too." Rebecca Mary pronounced it "hollow" with careful precision. Aunt Olivia would not approve of "holler." "And when you can't, you like to listen. But I s'posed listening to them hollow would be 'sociating. So I put the cotton in."

The joyous "hollowing" broke in waves of glee on Aunt Olivia's eardrums. It seemed to be assaulting her heart. Oddly, now it did not sound unmannerly and dreadful. It sounded nice and cheerful. A Plummer, even, might be happy like that.

"Cotton is a very strange ex - exper'ence, Thomas Jefferson," ran on the little voice. "At first you 'most can't stand it, but you get over the worst of it bymeby. Besides, we're getting 'most through now. Ain't that splendid, Thomas Jefferson? And it's pretty lucky, too, because Aunt 'Livia's birthday is getting very near. It -

it almost scares me. Doesn't it you? For I don't know how Aunt 'Livia looks when she's pleased - you think she'll look pleased, don't you, Thomas Jefferson? It's such a long quilt, and when you've sewed every stitch yourself - "

If Rebecca Mary had turned round then she would have seen how Aunt Olivia looked when she was pleased. But the little figure at the quilting-frame bent steadily to its task, only another soft sigh stealing into Aunt Olivia's uncottoned ears. Thomas Jefferson pecked his way towards the open door, and the lean figure there started back guiltily; Aunt Olivia did not want to be recognized.

"You there under the quilt, Thomas Jefferson?" The little voice put on tenderness. "Because I'm a-going to tell you something. Once Aunt 'Livia gave ME a birthday present and it was YOU. Such a little mite of a yellow chicken! That's why I'm making the quilt for Aunt 'Livia. It was three years ago; I've loved you ever since," added Rebecca Mary, simply.

For an instant Aunt Olivia stopped being a Plummer. A sob crept into her throat. "Rebecca! Rebecca Mary! Rebecca Mary Plummer!" she cried, involuntarily. Then she stepped back hastily, glad for the cotton in Rebecca Mary's ears. For the surprise - she must not spoil the child's hard-earned surprise. And, besides, Aunt Olivia wanted to be surprised.

It was a relief to get away. She could not look any longer at the picture in the great cobwebby barn - the gorgeous quilt spread out to its full extent, the empty scaffolds above Rebecca Mary stooping to her work, Thomas Jefferson pecking about the floor. Aunt Olivia

Annie Hamilton Donnell

was not old; through all the years ahead of her she would remember that picture.

She went straight to the southern boundary fence and looked across at the jubilant little Tony Trumbullses. The one in a red dress like Rebecca Mary's she singled out with a pointing finger. "YOU come here," she called. "I won't hurt you; no need to look scairt. Do you know who I am? I'm Rebecca Mary's aunt. You know who Rebecca Mary is, don't you?"

"Gracious!" shrilled the little red Tony Trumbull, which Aunt Olivia took for yes.

"Well, then, you know where I live. You see here - I want you all, the whole kit o' you, to come to my house tomorrow morning to see Rebecca Mary. I'm going to say it over again. Tomorrow morning, to see Rebecca Mary!" setting apart the syllables with the pointing finger. "You can play in my back yard," said Aunt Olivia, sublimely unconscious of slang.

The Bible Dream

Rebecca Mary sat on the kitchen steps, shelling peas and trying not to listen. She had begun a hummy little tune to help out, but in the interstices of rattling peas and the verses of the tune she could distinctly hear some of the things Aunt Olivia and the Caller were saying. This was one of the things:

"She's offered a reward, but *I* don't calculate there's much chance she'll ever see it again."

A sigh followed. The voice was the Caller's, the sigh Aunt Olivia's.

"It's queer where it ever went to!" Aunt Olivia's voice.

"Yes, it's all o' QUEER," the Caller's, with mysterious hints in it that made Rebecca Mary, out on the doorsteps, shudder suddenly and forget where she was in the tune. Oh, oh, dear, did they s'pose - they couldn't s'pose it had been STOLEN?

Rebecca Mary's little hard brown hand stopped halfway to the pea-basket and fell limply at her side on the doorstep. It made a little thud as it fell. Rebecca Mary's horrified gaze wandered out into the glare of sunshine where wandered Thomas Jefferson, stepping daintily, hunting bugs. That was his day's work.

Annie Hamilton Donnell

Thomas Jefferson was a hard worker.

The voices went on, but Rebecca Mary did not heed them now; she was looking at Thomas Jefferson, but she did not see him. Not until - it happened. On a sudden Thomas Jefferson, forgetful of dignity, made a swoop for something that glittered in the grass. Then Rebecca Mary saw him - then started to her feet with an inarticulate little cry, while in her honest brown eyes the horror grew. Oh, oh, dear, what was that Thomas Jefferson had swooped for? For a brief instant it had glittered in the grass - Rebecca Mary knew in her soul that it had glittered.

Thomas Jefferson stretched his sheeny neck, curved it ridiculously, and crowed. It sounded like a crow of triumph; that was the way he crowed when the bug had been a delicious one.

The Caller was coming out, Aunt Olivia with her. Rebecca Mary could hear the crackle of their starched skirts; Aunt Olivia's crackled loudest. Rebecca Mary had always had a queer feeling that Aunt Olivia herself was starched. There had never been a time when she could not remember her carrying her head very stiffly and straight and never bending her back. Nobody else in the world, Rebecca Mary reflected proudly, could pick up a pin without bending. SHE couldn't, herself, even after she had privately practiced a good deal.

"Good afternoon, Rebecca Mary; you out here?" the Caller nodded pleasantly. Folks had such queer ways of saying things. How could you say good afternoon to anybody if she WASN'T here?

"Didn't you hear Mrs. Dixey, Rebecca Mary? I guess

you've forgot your manners," came in Aunt Olivia's crisp tones.

"Oh yes'm, I have. I mean I DID. Yes'm, thank you, I'm out here," quavered Rebecca Mary. She was not afraid of the Caller and she had never been afraid of Aunt Olivia, but the horror that was settling round her heart made her clear little voice unsteady. Her eyes were still following Thomas Jefferson on his mincing travels about the yard. The sunshine was on his splendid white coat, but Rebecca Mary felt no pride in him.

"Ain't that the han'somest rooster! You ought to show him at the fair, I declare! See how his feathers glisten in the sun!"

"Thomas Jefferson belongs to Rebecca Mary," Aunt Olivia said, briefly. "She raised him."

"My! Well, he's han'some enough. Ain't it amusing how a nice-feeling rooster like that will go stepping round as if he felt about too toppy to live! He'd ought to wear diamonds."

"Oh, oh, dear, please don't!" breathed Rebecca Mary, softly, but neither of the women heard her.

"Well, well, I must be going. I've made a regular visit. But I tell John when I get away from home, it feels so good I STAY! 'I don't get away any too often,' I says, 'and I guess I've earnt the right.' Well, I must be going if I'm ever going to! Good-bye, Miss Plummer - good-bye, Rebecca Mary. All is, I hope Mis' Avery's boarder'll find her diamond, don't you? But I don't calculate she will. Well, good afternoon. She hadn't

Annie Hamilton Donnell

ought to have wore the ring, when she knew it was loose in the setting like that. Some folks are just that careless! Well - "

But Rebecca Mary did not hear the rest of the Caller's leave-taking. She had slipped away to Thomas Jefferson out in the sun.

"Oh, come here - come here with me!" she cried, intensely. "Come out behind the barn where we can talk. I've got to say something to you that's awful! I've GOT to, you've got to listen, Thomas Jefferson."

It was still and terribly hot in the treeless glare behind the barn, but it was all in the day's work to Thomas Jefferson. Behind the barn was a beautiful place for bugs.

"Listen! Oh, you poor dear, you've got to listen!" Rebecca Mary cried. "You've got to stop hunting for bugs - and don't you dare to crow! If you crow, Thomas Jefferson, it will break my heart. I don't s'pose you know what you've done - I don't know as you'vedone it - but there's something awful happened. Oh, Thomas Jefferson, it glittered - I saw it glitter!" Suddenly Rebecca Mary stooped and gathered Thomas Jefferson into her arms. She held him with a passionate clasp against her flat little calico breast. He was HERS. He was all the intimate friend she had ever had. He had been her little downy baby and slept in her hand. She had fed him and watched him grow and been proud of him. He was her all.

"Oh, Thomas Jefferson, Thomas Jefferson, what was it that glittered in the grass? Tell me and I'll believe you. Say it was a little piece o' glass and I'll put you down and go get you some corn, and we'll never speak of it again. But don't look at me like that - don't look at me like that! You look - GUILTY!"

She rocked him in her arms. In her soul she knew what it was that had glittered. But in Thomas Jefferson's soul - oh, they could not blame Thomas Jefferson!

"You haven't got any soul, poor dear; poor dear, you haven't got any soul, and you can't be guilty without a soul. They couldn't - hang - you." Her voice sank to the merest whisper. She tightened her clasp on the great, soft body and smoothed the soft feathers with a tender, tremulous little hand.

"The Lord didn't put anything in you but a stomach and a - a gizzard. He left your soul out and you're not to blame for that. I don't blame you, Thomas Jefferson, and of course the Lord don't. But Mrs. Avery's boarder - oh, oh, dear, I'm afraid Mrs. Avery's boarder will! You mustn't tell - I mean I mustn't. Nobody must know what it was that glittered in the grass. Do you want to be - searched?

"You know 'xactly where she sat over to this house yesterday morning, when she went by - and how she said you were too sweet for anything - and how she flew her hand round with - with IT on it. You know as well as I do. And it was loose, the di'mond-stone was loose. We didn't either of us know that. We're not to blame if things are loose, and you're not to blame for not having any soul. But oh, oh, dear, how dreadfully it makes us both feel! You'd better give up crowing, Thomas Jefferson; I feel just as if you'd let it out if you crew."

Annie Hamilton Donnell

At tea Rebecca Mary played with her spoon, while her berries swam, untasted, in their yellow sea of cream. Aunt Olivia remonstrated.

"Why don't you eat your supper, child?" she asked, sharply. Rebecca Mary was always glad when she said child instead of Rebecca Mary, for then the sharpness did not cut. She was feeling now for the glasses up in her thin gray hair. Aunt Olivia could see everything through those glasses and it made Rebecca Mary tremble to think - oh, oh, dear, suppose she should see the secret hidden in Rebecca Mary's soul! It seemed as if Aunt Olivia trained the glasses directly upon the corner where the secret glittered in the gra - was hidden in Rebecca Mary's troubled little soul. But this is what Aunt Olivia said:

"It's your stomach. What you need is a good dose of camomile tea to tone you up. I didn't give you any this spring, for a wonder. Now you go right up to bed and I'll set some to steeping. Does it hurt you any?"

"Oh yes'm," murmured Rebecca Mary, sadly, but she meant her soul and Aunt Olivia meant her stomach. She mounted the steep stairs to her little eavesdropping room and slipped her small spare body out of her clothes into her scant little nightgown. It was rather a relief to go to bed. If she could have been sure that Thomas Jefferson - but, no, Thomas Jefferson was not in bed. As Rebecca Mary lay and waited for her camomile tea she was certain she could hear him stepping about under the window. Once he came directly under and "crew," and then Rebecca Mary hid her head in the pillow for he was letting it out.

"Cock-a-doodle-do - ooo,   did-you-see-me-swoo-oo-

OOP-it-up?" crowed Thomas Jefferson, under the window. Rebecca Mary with her eyes pillow-deep could see him stretching his neck and letting it out. It seemed to her everybody could hear him - Aunt Olivia downstairs, steeping camomile 'blows, and Mrs. Avery's boarder across the fields.

"Aunt Olivia," whispered Rebecca Mary, while she sipped her bitter tea a little later, "how much - I suppose precious things cost a great deal, don't they?"

"My grief!" Aunt Olivia set down the bowl and felt of Rebecca Mary's temples, then of her wrists. The child was out of her head.

"Di'mond-stones like - like that boarder's - I suppose those cost a great deal? As much as - how much as, Aunt Olivia?"

"My grief, don't you worry about any di'mond-stones! YOU haven't lost any. What you'll lose will be your health, if you don't swallow down the rest o' this tea and go right to sleep like a good girl! No, no, I'm not going to answer any questions. Drink this; swallow it down."

Rebecca Mary swallowed it down, but she did not go right to sleep like a good girl. She lay on the hard little bed and thought of many things, or of one thing many times. Over and over, wearily, drearily, until the sin of Thomas Jefferson became her sin. She adopted it.

When at last she dropped to sleep it was to dream a Bible dream. Usually Rebecca Mary liked to dream Bible dreams, but not this one. This one was different. This one was of Abraham and Isaac. She thought she

Annie Hamilton Donnell

was right there and saw Abraham build the little altar and offer up - no, it wasn't Isaac! It was Thomas Jefferson. And the Abraham in her dream was turning into HER. The flowing white robes were dwindling to a little scant white nightgown. She stood a little way off and saw herself offering up Thomas Jefferson. It was a dreadful dream.

The night was a perfectly black one, the kind that Rebecca Mary was afraid of . It was the only thing in the world she had ever been afraid of - a black night. But after the dream she got up stealthily and slipped through the blackness, out to Thomas Jefferson. It was only out to the little lean-to shed, but it seemed a very long way to Rebecca Mary. The blackness pressed up against her, she put out her little, trembling hands and pushed through it.

"Thomas Jefferson! Thomas Jefferson!" she called softly. But he was a sound sleeper, she remembered; she would have to find him and wake him. In the darkness she felt about on Thomas Jefferson's perch for Thomas Jefferson . When the little groping hand came upon something very soft and warm, the other hand went up to join it, and together they lifted Thomas Jefferson down. He gave a protesting croak, and then, because he was acquainted with the clasp of the two small hands, and night or day liked it, he went back to his interrupted dreams and said not another word. Thomas Jefferson had never dreamed a Bible dream - never heard of Abraham or Isaac, had no soul to be disquieted.

With her burden against her breast Rebecca Mary pushed back through the darkness, up to the black little room under the eaves. She felt about for her little carpet-covered shoe box and gently crowded the great white bulk into it. Then she crept back into bed and lay on the outer edge with her loving, light little hand on Thomas Jefferson's feathers. The trouble in her burdened soul poured itself out.

"Oh, Thomas Jefferson," she whispered down to the heap of soft feathers, "I'm going to smooth you this way all night for tomorrow you die!" Her voice even in a whisper had a solemn, inspired note. "There's no other way; you'll have to make up your mind to be willing. It's going to break my heart, and, oh, I'm afraid it will break yours! I'm afraid it will kill us both!"

Thomas Jefferson uttered a mournful little croaky sound that might have been "ET TU, BRUTE?" It pierced Rebecca Mary's breast. "There, hush, poor dear, poor dear, and rest. You'll need all your sleep," she crooned softly and brokenly. "Tomorrow morning I'll give you some beautiful corn, and then - and then I'm going to take you to Mrs. Avery's boarder and tell her the worst. I'm going to give you up, Thomas Jefferson; and I'm the best friend you've got in the world! But I've got to, I've got to - I've got to! It's been revealed to me in a dream. There was a man once in the Bible, named Abraham, and there was his dearly beloved little boy named Isaac. And now here's me named Rebecca Mary, and dearly beloved you named Thomas Jefferson. Oh, I don't suppose you can understand; I suppose you're asleep. You'll never know how it feels to give up your dearly belovedest, but oh, oh, dear, you'll know how it feels to be given up! You'll be one o' the blessed martyrs, Thomas Jefferson - doesn't that comfort you a little speck? Oh, why don't you wake up and be comforted?

Annie Hamilton Donnell

"The Lord excused Abraham, after all. But this isn't the Lord, it's Mrs. Avery's boarder. I'm afraid she isn't the Lord's kind - I'm afraid not, Thomas Jefferson. I don't dare to let you hope; I've got to prepare you for the worst."

She caught up the big, white fellow with sudden, irresistible yearning and sat up with him and rocked him back and forth in her arms. She began a muffled, sad little tune like a wail. The words were terrible words.

"I'll hold you in my arms. I'll rock you - rock you - rock you. For tomorrow, oh, to-MOR-row you - must - die! Aber-a-ham offered Isaac, and *I* -MUST OFFER YOU."

Over and over, then tenderly she lowered Thomas Jefferson to the shoe box again.

When Aunt Olivia came up in the morning, vaguely alarmed because it was so late and no Rebecca Mary stirring, she had news to tell. Someone going by had told her something.

"Well, that woman's found her 'di'mond-stone,' - how are you feeling this morning, child? It was in her pocket where she'd put her hand in and felt round! So all that fuss for noth - "

Suddenly Aunt Olivia stopped, for without warning, out of a box at the bedside stalked a great white rooster and flew to the foot board and "crew":

"Cock-a-doodle-do-ooo!

It was glass that glittered in the grass,

And all the time I knew-oo-ooo!"

"My grief?" Aunt Olivia gasped.

The Cookbook Diary

Rebecca Mary decided to keep a diary. It was not an inspiration, though it was rather like one in its suddenness. Of course she had always known that Aunt Olivia kept a diary. When she was very small she had stretched a-tiptoe and with little pointing forefinger counted rows and rows of little black books that Aunt Olivia had "kept." Each little black book had its year-label pasted neatly on the back. Rebecca Mary breathcd deep breaths of awe, there were so many of them. There must be so much weather in those little black books - so many pleasant days, rainy days, storms, and snows!

It was Rebecca Mary who remembered that it was Tuesday, and that it had showered a little Wednesday - shone Thursday - showered again on Friday. Rebecca Mary was the jog to Aunt Olivia's memory. It gave her now, at the beginning of her own diary career, an experienced feeling, as if she knew already how to keep a diary. It made it seem a much simpler matter to begin.

And then, of course, the minister's littlest little boy - really it was the minister's littlest little boy who had started Rebecca Mary. He had volunteered a peep into his own diary, and made whispered explanations and suggestions. He let Rebecca Mary read some of the entries: "MUNDY, plesent and good. TUSDY, rany and bad. WENSDY, sum plesent and not good enuf to hirt. THIRSDY " but he had hastily withdrawn the book at "Thirsdy," and a tidal-wave of warm red blood had flowed up over his little brown ears and in around all the little brown islands of his freckles. So Rebecca Mary had begun hastily to talk of other things. For the minister's littlest little boy had explained that the first Statement in each entry referred to the weather and the second to the deportment of the writer, and Rebecca Mary had remarked a sympathetic resemblance between the two statements. She had caught a fleeting glimpse of the weather part of "Thirsdy" - she could guess the rest. Better let the curtain fall on "Thirsdy." On her way home Rebecca Mary decided to keep a diary herself. Her first day's record had been a good deal like the "Mundy" of the minister's littlest little boy, only there were more a's in the weather. After that, little by little, she branched out into a certain originality - the Rebecca Mary sort. If she had not been hampered by circumstances, it would have been easier to be original. The most hampering circumstance was the cookbook itself, which she was driven to use in her new undertaking. There was room on the blank leaves and above and below the recipes for cake and pudding and pie. The book was one Aunt Olivia had given her long ago to draw impossible pictures in.

In the beginning Rebecca Mary tried pasting pieces of "empty" paper over the pies and puddings and cakes, but the empty paper was too transparent. In rather startling places things were liable to show through.

As: "SUNDAY. - It rained a level teaspoonful. Aunt Olivia and I went to church. The text was thou shalt not steal 1 cups of sour milk - " Rebecca Mary got no farther than that. She was a little appalled at the result thus far, and hastily turned a page and began again in a blank space where no intrusive pudding could break through and corrupt. Thereafter she wrote above and below the recipes and pasted no more thin veils over them. It seemed safer.

Aunt Olivia, apparently oblivious to what was going on, yet saw and did not disapprove. It was to be expected that the child should come into her inheritance sometime, early or late. If early - well.

"It's the Plummer in her. All the Plummers have kept diaries," Aunt Olivia mused, knitting stolidly on while the child stooped painfully to her self-imposed task. The quaint resemblance to herself at her own diary-writing did not escape her, and she smiled a little in the Aunt Olivia way that scarcely stirred her lips. Aunt Olivia smiled oftener now when she looked at the child. She was "failing" a little, Plummerly. Between the two of them, little Plummer and big, stretched of late a tie woven of sheets and a gorgeous quilt of a thousand bits. It was not very visible to the naked eye, but they were both rather shyly conscious that it was there. They would never be quite so far apart again.

Rebecca Mary took her diary out to the haunts of Thomas Jefferson and read aloud selections to him, with an odd, conscious little air, as though she were graduating. The great white fellow was a sympathetic auditor, if silence and extreme gravity count. Only once did he ever make comments, and Rebecca Mary could never quite make up her mind whether he laughed then or applauded. When a great white rooster elongates his neck, crooks it ridiculously, flaps his wings and crows, it's hard telling exactly what feeling prompts him. But Rebecca reasoned from past experience and her faith in him - he had never laughed at her before. It was applause. The especial entry which evoked it was the one that first mentioned an allowance.

"'THURSDAY. - I think I'm going to - '" read Rebecca Mary slowly; and it was significant that on this Thursday there was no weather. "'I havent desided - I don't KNOW, but I think I'm going to ask Aunt Olivia to pay me 5 cents a weak. Rhoda says you call it an alowance, and I supose she knows. She is the minnister's daughter. She has 10 cents a weak unless shes bad and then she pays the minnister an alowance. He charges her 1 cent a sin and he gives it to somebody who is indignant - I think Rhoda said indignant. Then I should think he would give it back to Rhoda. I shant only ask Aunt Olivia for 5 cents - I think she will be more likely. I havent desided but I THINK I shall ask her tomorrow after her knap. After knaps you are more rested and maybe things dont look just as they do before knaps.

"'FRIDAY. - I think Ide better wait untill tomorrow. Her knap was rather short. Ive desided to say you needent alow but 4 if 5 is too mutch. If she alows Im going to buy me some crimpers. Rhodas curls natchurally but she says you can crimp it if it doesent. I have begun to look at myself in the glass and it fritens me - I guess there ought to be a gh in that - to see how homebly I am. I wonder if it doesent kind of scare Aunt Olivia. Prehaps if I was pretty like Rhoda she would call me darling and dear instead of Rebecca Mary. I dont blame her mutch because I LOOK like Rebecca Mary.

"'SATURDAY. - I think Sunday will be the best time to ask her, just after she gets home from meeting and has rolled her bonnet strings up, espesialy if the minnister preaches on the Lord lovething a cheerful giver. I am hopeing he will. If I dont get the crimpers Ime going to give up looking in the glass. For I think Ime growing homeblyer right along. Theres something the matter with my nose. Rhodas doesent run up hill. I never thought about noses before. Aunt Olivias is a little quear too but I like it became its Aunt Olivias nose. I wish I knew if Aunt Olivia liked mine. I wish we were better akquainted.

"'SUNDAY. - I wish the Lord had created mine curly because I dont dass to ask Aunt Olivia. I don't dass to, so there. It scares my throat. I supose its because aunts arnt mothers - seems as if youd dass to ask your MOTHER. I hate to be scart on acount of being a Plummer. Im afraid Im the only Plummer that ever was - '"

The reading suddenly stopped here. This was Sunday, and the last entry was fresh from Rebecca Mary's pencil.

"Thomas Jefferson!" stormed Rebecca Mary, in a little gust of passion, "don't you ever TELL I was scared! As long as you live! - cross your heart! - oh, I wish I hadn't read that part to you! You're a Plummer too, and you never were scared, and you can't understand - "

The diary was clutched to Rebecca Mary's little flat breast, and with a swirl of starched Sunday skirts the child was gone. She went straight to Aunt Olivia. Red spots of shame flamed in both sallow little cheeks; resolution sat astride her little uphill nose. She could not bear to go, but it was easier than being ashamed. The pointing fingers of all the Plummers pushed her on. Go she must, or be a coward. Long ago - it seemed long to Rebecca Mary - she had stood up straight and stanch and refused to make any more sheets. Was that little girl who had dared, THIS little girl who was afraid? Should that little girl be ashamed of this one?

"Aunt Olivia," steadily, though Rebecca Mary's heart was pounding hard - "Aunt Olivia, are - are you well off?"

She had not meant to begin like that, but afterwards she was glad that she had.

"My grief!" Aunt Olivia ejaculated in her surprise. What would the child ask next? "Am I well off? If you mean rich, no, I ain't."

"Oh! Then you're - why, I didn't think about your being poor! I shouldn't have thought of asking - that makes a great difference. I never thought of THAT!"

She was off before Aunt Olivia had fully recovered her breath, and the stumping of her heavy little shoes going upstairs was the only distinctly audible sound. In her own room Rebecca Mary stopped, panting.

Oh, I'm glad I didn't get as far as ASKING!" she breathed aloud. "I never thought about her being poor - of course then I wouldn't ask!"

But she squared her shoulders and stood up, straight and unashamed. For she had vindicated herself. She had been ready to ask. She could look that other little girl of the sheets in the face. The Other Little Girl was there, coming to meet her as she advanced to the little looking glass above the table. But Rebecca Mary waved her back peremptorily.

"Go right back!" she said. "I only came to tell you I wasn't a coward - that's all. Good-bye. For I'm not coming any more. You're sorry I'm homely, and I'm sorry you are, but it doesn't do any good for us to look at each other and groan. It will make us unsatisfied. So I shall turn you back to the wall - good-bye."

But for a very ***?*** instant they looked sadly into each other's little lean brown-yellow faces. It was a brief ceremony of farewell. "Good-bye," smiled Rebecca Mary, bravely. And the lips of The Other Little Girl moved as though saying it too. The Other Little Girl smiled. And neither of them knew that just then she was beautiful.

Aunt Olivia was trying to meet her own courage test. She had been trying a good many days. Duty - stern, unswerving duty - bade her inspect Rebecca Mary's little cookbook diary. Should she not know - ought she not to know the thoughts that were brewing in the child's mind? How else could she bring her up properly?

"Read it," Duty said," find out. Are you afraid?"

"I'm ashamed," groaned Aunt Olivia. "Do you think Rebecca Mary would read my diary?"

"Is Rebecca Mary bringing you up?"

Aunt Olivia sometimes thought so. The puzzle that she had begun to try to solve when Rebecca Mary's white, death-struck mother had laid her baby in Aunt Olivia's unaccustomed arms was getting a little more difficult every day. Some days Aunt Olivia wondered if she ought to give it up. Oh, this bringing up - this bringing up of little children!

"If I must," groaned Aunt Olivia, and got as far as taking the little diary in her hands. But she got no farther. She laid it gently down again.

"I can't," she said, firmly, but she could not look Duty in the face as she said it. She had always listened to Duty before.

"You know you ought to - "

"Yes, I know, but I can't! It seems a shameful thing to do. I'm sure I've tried often enough - you know I've tried - "

"I know - that was good practice. Now stop trying and read it!"

Aunt Olivia flamed up. "I tell you I won't! It's a shameful thing. If I found Rebecca Mary reading one of my diaries, I should send her to bed - "

"Read hers and go to bed yourself. It's your duty to read it. When you bring up a child - "

"I never will again!"

Aunt Olivia read it, with the relentless grip of Duty holding her to the task. But flame spots crept up through the sallow of her thin cheeks and made what atonement they could.

It did not take long, though some of the pages she read twice. The weatherless week, when Rebecca Mary had put off her "asking" from day to day, Aunt Olivia went back to the third time. When she closed the little book it was not a Plummer face she lifted it to and laid it against for the space of a breath - a Plummer face would not have been wet.

Then she Whirled upon Duty. "Well, I've done it - I hope you're satisfied!"

"It had to be done," calm Duty responded. "If you think it will make you feel any better, you can send yourself to bed."

"I'm going to," sighed Aunt Olivia, slipping away to her room. A strange little yearning was upon her to hunt up Rebecca Mary and call her darling and dear. But in her heart she knew she should not have the courage to do it. Here was another Plummer coward!

"Why are some people made like me?" she thought - "so it kills 'em to say anything anyways tenderish. Seems to be too much for their vocal organs - they'd rather do a week's washing!"

Other thoughts came to Aunt Olivia as she lay on her bed, doing her whimsical penance for violating the sanctity of the little old cookbook. She was not comfortable. It was a hard bed - nothing was soft of Aunt Olivia's. She moved about on it uneasily.

"When they're dead, we're willing enough to say tenderish things to 'em," her musings ran. "We wish we HAD then. I suppose if Rebecca Mary was - "

She got no farther for the sudden horror that was upon her - that sent her to her feet and to the door. But there she stopped in the blessed relief that drifted in to her on a child's laugh. Somewhere out there Rebecca Mary was laughing in her subdued, sweet way. A cracked, shrill crow followed - Thomas Jefferson was laughing too.

Rebecca Mary was not dead. There was time to say a "tenderish" thing to her before she lay - before that. Aunt Olivia shut her eyes resolutely to the vision that had intruded upon her musings. It was Rebecca Mary who was laughing somewhere out there that she wanted to see.

The next day was Sunday, and in the quiet of the long afternoon Rebecca Mary read aloud again to Thomas Jefferson. It was from the little cookbook diary. Thomas Jefferson was pecking about the long grass of the orchard.

"Oh, listen!" cried Rebecca Mary, her eyes unwontedly shining. "Listen to this, Thomas Jefferson!

"'SATURDAY. - Wind northwest by Mrs. Tupper's Weather vain. Something happened yesterday. Aunt Olivia didn't say it, but she most did. She came right out of her bedroom and I saw it in her face! "Dear" - "darling," - they were both there, and she was looking at me! Nobody EVER looked "dear" "darling" at me before. I suppose my mother would have. If I hadent had another mother I think I should like to have had Aunt Olivia.

"'You feel that way more after you get akquainted. When I get VERY akquainted prehaps I shall tell Aunt

Olivia. Its quear, I think, how it isent as easy to say some things as it is to think them. You can wright them easier too. I am glad Ime keeping a diary because I can wright about yesterday and what happenned. I shall read it to my grand children - to be continude.

"'SUNDAY' - that's today, Thomas Jefferson, - 'SUNDAY. - This is yesterday continude, because there was too mutch for one day. Something else beutiful happenned. My Aunt Olivia said to me as folows, I have desided to pay you a weakly alowance of 10 cents a weak Rebecca Mary. And I never asked her to. And she never said anything about charging me for my sins. I was going to ask her but I found out she was poor. That was a mistake, she isent. She must be SOME well of I think for 10 cents seams a great deal to have of your own every weak. But I shant buy crimpers. Ime going to buy a present for Aunt Olivia byamby. Ime very happy. I wish I knew how to spell hooray.'"

Suddenly Rebecca Mary was on her feet, waving the cookbook jubilantly.

"Hoo-ray! Hoo-ray! Thomas Jefferson!" she shouted, surprising the gentle Sunday calm. She surprised Thomas Jefferson, too, but he was equal to the occasion - Thomas Jefferson was a gentleman.

"Hoo-ra-a-a-ay!" he crowed, splendidly, with a fine effect of clapping his hands.

This time there could be no doubt. This was applause.

The Bereavement

Thomas Jefferson was losing his appetite. Even Aunt Olivia noticed it, but it did not worry her as it did Rebecca Mary.

"He's always had as many appetites as a cat's got lives - he's got eight good ones left," she said, calmly.

But Rebecca Mary was not calm. It seemed to her that Thomas Jefferson was getting thinner every day.

"Oh, I can feel your bones!" she cried, in distress. "Your bones are coming through, you poor, dear Thomas Jefferson! Won't you eat just one more kernel of corn - just this one for Rebecca Mary? I'd do it for you. Shut your eyes and swallow it right down and you'll never know it."

That day Thomas Jefferson listened to pleading, but not the next day - nor the next. He went about dispiritedly, and the last few times that he crowed it made Rebecca Mary cry. Even Aunt Olivia shook her head.

"I could do it better than that myself," she said, soberly.

Rebecca Mary hunted bugs and angleworms and

Annie Hamilton Donnell

arranged them temptingly in rows, but the big, white rooster passed them by with a feeble peck or two. Bits of bread failed to tempt him, or even his favorite cooky crumbs. His eighth appetite departed - his seventh, sixth, fifth, fourth.

"He lost his third one yesterday," lamented Rebecca Mary, "and today he's lost his second. It's pretty bad when he hasn't only one left, Aunt Olivia."

"Pretty bad," nodded Aunt Olivia. She was stirring up a warm mush. When Rebecca Mary had gone upstairs she took it to Thomas Jefferson and commanded him to eat. He was beyond coaxing - perhaps he needed commanding.

Rebecca Mary thought Aunt Olivia did not care, and it added a new sting to her pain. There was that time that Aunt Olivia said she wished the Lord hadn't ever created roosters - Thomas Jefferson had just scratched up her pansy seeds. And the time when she wished Thomas Jefferson was dead; did she wish that now? Was she - was she glad he was going to be dead?

For Rebecca Mary had given up hope. She was not reconciled, but she was sure. She spent all her spare time with the big, gaunt, pitiful fellow, trying to make his last days easier. She knew he liked to have her with him.

"You do, don't you, dear?" she said. She had never called him "dear" before. She realized sadly that this was her last chance. "You do like to have me here, don't you? You'd rather? Don't try to crow - just nod your head a little if you do." And the big, white fellow's head had nodded a little, she was sure. She put out her loving little brown hand and caressed it. "I knew you did, dear. Oh, Thomas Jefferson, Thomas Jefferson, don't die! PLEASE don't - think of the good times we'll have if you won't! Think of the - the grasshoppers - the bugs, Thomas Jefferson - the cookies! Won't you think? - won't you try to be a little bit hungry?"

Rebecca Mary knew what it was to be hungry and not be able to eat, but to be able to eat and not be hungry - this was away and beyond her experience. The sad puzzle of it she could not solve.

One day the minister had a rather surprising summons to perform his priestly functions. The summoner was Rebecca Mary. She appeared like a sombre little shadow in his sunny sermon room. The minister's wife ushered her in, and in the brief instant of opening the door and announcing her name flashed him a warning glance. He had been acquainted so long with her glances that he was able to interpret this one with considerable accuracy. "All right," he glanced back. No, he would not smile - yes, he would remember that it was Rebecca Mary.

"Do what she asks you," flashed the minister's wife's glance.

"All right," flashed the minister. Then the door closed.

"Thomas Jefferson is dying," Rebecca Mary began, hurriedly. "I came to see if you'd come."

In spite of himself the minister gasped. Then, as the situation dawned clearly upon him, his mouth corners began - in spite of themselves - to curve upward. But in time he remembered the minister's wife, and drew them back to their centres of gravity. He waited a little. It was safer.

"Aunt Olivia isn't at home and I'm glad. She doesn't care. Perhaps she would laugh. Oh, I know," appealed Rebecca Mary, piteously, "I know he's a rooster! It isn't because I don't know - but he's FOLKS to me! You needn't do anything but just smooth his feathers a little and say the Lord bless you. I thought perhaps you'd come and do that. *I* could, but I wanted you to, because you're a minister. I thought - I thought perhaps you'd try and forget he's a rooster."

"I will," the minister said, gently. Now his lips were quite grave. He took Rebecca Mary's hand and went with her.

"He's a good man," murmured the minister's wife, watching them go. She had known he would go.

"He was one of my parishioners," the minister was saying for the comforting of Rebecca Mary. Unconsciously he used the past tense, as one speaks of those close to death. It was well enough, for already big, gaunt, white Thomas Jefferson was in the past tense.

Rebecca Mary chronicled the sad event in her diary:

"Tomas Jefferson passed away at ten minutes of three this afternoon blessed are them that die in the Lord. The minnister did not get here in time. I wish I had asked him to run for he is a very good minnister and would have. He helped me berry him in the cold cold ground and we sang a him. I dident ask him to pray because he was only a rooster, but he was folks to me. I loved him. It is very lonesome. I dred wakening up tomorrow because he always crowed under my window. The Lord gaveth and the Lord has taken away."

This last Rebecca Mary erased once, but she wrote it again after a moment's thought. For, she reasoned, it was the Lord part of Aunt Olivia which had given Thomas Jefferson to her. In the primitive little creed of Rebecca Mary every one had a Lord part, but some people's was very small. Not Aunt Olivia's - she had never gauged Aunt Olivia's Lord part; it would not have been consistent with her ideas of loyalty.

It was very lonely, as Rebecca Mary had known it would be. At best her life had never been overfull of companionships, and the sudden taking-off - it seemed sudden, as all deaths do - of Thomas Jefferson was hard to bear. Strange how blank a space one great, white rooster can leave behind him!

The yard and the orchard seemed full of blank spaces, though in a way Thomas Jefferson's soul seemed to frequent his old beloved haunts. Rebecca Mary could not see it pecking daintily about, but she felt it was there.

"His soul isn't dead," she persisted, gently. She clung to the comfort of that. And one morning she thought she heard again Thomas Jefferson's old, cheery greeting to the sunrise. The sound she thought she heard woke her instantly. Was it Thomas Jefferson's soul crowing?

"Aunt Olivia isent sorry," chronicled the diary, sadly.

Annie Hamilton Donnell

"Prehaps shes glad. Once she wished the Lord had forgot to create roosters. But she was ever kind to Tomas Jefferson, considdering the seeds he scrached up. That was his besittingest sin and I know he is sorry now. I wish Aunt Olivia was sorry."

Nothing was ever said between the two about Rebecca Mary's loss, but Aunt Olivia recognized the keenness of it to the child. She worried a little about it; it reminded her of that other time of worry when Rebecca Mary and she had nearly starved. Sheets and roosters - there were so many worries in the world.

That other time she went to the minister, this time to the minister's wife. One afternoon she went and carried her work.

"You know about children," she began, without loss of time. "What happens when they lose their appetite over a dead rooster?"

"Thomas Jefferson?" breathed the minister's wife, softly.

"Yes - he's dead and buried, and she's mourning for him. I set three tarts on for dinner today, and I set three tarts AWAY after dinner. Rebecca Mary is fond of tarts. What should you do if it was Rhoda?"

"Oh - -Rhoda - why, I think I should get her another rooster, or a cat or something, to get her mind off. But Rhoda isn't Rebecca Mary - "

Aunt Olivia folded up her work. She got up briskly.

"They've got a white rooster down to the Trumbullses'," she said. "I guess I better go right down now; Tony Trumbull is liable to be at home just before supper. I'm very much obliged to you for your advice."

"Did I advise her?" murmured the minister's wife, watching the resolute swing of Aunt Olivia's skirts as she strode away. "I was going to tell her that what would cure my Rhoda might not cure Rebecca Mary. Well, I hope it will work," but she was sure it wouldn't. She had grown a little acquainted with Rebecca Mary.

It was the new, white rooster crowing, instead of the soul of Thomas Jefferson. Rebecca Mary found out after she had dressed and gone downstairs. Soon after that she appeared in the kitchen doorway with an armful of snowy feathers. Aunt Olivia, over her muffin pans, eyed her with secret delight. The cure was working sooner than she had dared to expect.

"This is the Tony Trumbullses' rooster; if I hurry I guess I can carry him back before breakfast," Rebecca Mary said from the doorway. "I'll run, Aunt Olivia."

"Carry him back!" Aunt Olivia's muffin spoon dropped into the bowl of creamy batter. One look at Rebecca Mary convinced her that the cure had not begun to work. Imperceptibly she stiffened. "He ain't anybody's but mine. I've bought him," she explained, briefly. "You set him down and feed him with these crumbs - he ain't human if he don't like cloth-o'-gold cake."

But the child in the doorway, after gently releasing the great fellow, drew away quietly. The second look at her face convinced Aunt Olivia that the cure would never work.

"You feed him, please, Aunt Olivia," Rebecca Mary said; "I - couldn't. I'll stir the muffins up."

Nothing further was ever said about keeping the Tony Trumbull rooster. He pecked about the place in unrestrained freedom until the morning work was done, and then Aunt Olivia carried him home in her apron.

"I concluded not to keep him - he'd likely be homesick," she said, with a qualm of conscience; for the big, white fellow had certainly shown no signs of homesickness. But she could not explain and reveal the secret places of Rebecca Mary's heart. Aunt Olivia, too, had her ideas of loyalty.

In the diary there occurred brief mention of the episode: "The Tony Trumbull rooster has been here. I could eat him - that's how I feel about the Tony Trumbull rooster.

"I never could have eatten Tomas Jefferson but once and then it would have broken my heart but I was starveing. Aunt Olivia took him back."

Thomas Jefferson's grave was kept green. Rebecca Mary took her stents down into the orchard and sat beside it, sadly stitching. She kept it heaped with wild flowers and poppies from her own rows. Aunt Olivia's flowers she never touched. The bitterness of Aunt Olivia's not being sorry - perhaps being glad - rankled in her sore little soul. It would have helped - oh yes, it would have helped.

Aunt Olivia worried on. It seemed to her that all Rebecca Mary's meals in one meal would not have kept a kitten alive - and that reminded her. She would try a kitten. The minister's wife had said a rooster or a cat. A white kitten, she decided, though she could scarcely have told why.

The kitten was better, but it was not a cure. Rebecca Mary took the little creature to her breast and told it her grief for Thomas Jefferson and cried her Thomas Jefferson tears into its soft, white fur. In that way, at any rate, it was a success.

"Maybe I shall love you some day," she whispered, "but I can't yet, while Thomas Jefferson is fresh. He's all I have room for. He was my intimate friend - when your intimate friend is dead you can't love anybody else right away." But she apologized to the little cat gently - she felt that an apology was due it.

"You see how it is, little, white cat," she said. "I shall have to ask you to wait. But if I ever have a second love, I promise it will be you. You're a great DEAL comfortinger than that Tony Trumbull rooster! I could love you this minute if I had never loved Thomas Jefferson. Do you feel like waiting?"

The little, white cat waited. And Aunt Olivia waited. She made tempting dishes for Rebecca Mary's meals, and put a ruffle into her nightgown neck and sleeves - Rebecca Mary had always yearned for ruffles.

"I don't believe she sees 'em. She don't know they're there," groaned Aunt Olivia, impotently. "She don't see anything but Thomas Jefferson, and I don't know as she ever will!"

But Rebecca Mary saw the ruffles and fluted them

Annie Hamilton Donnell

between her brown little fingers admiringly. She tried once or twice to go and thank Aunt Olivia, and got as far as her bedroom door. But the bitterness in her heart stayed her hand from turning the knob. If Aunt Olivia had only known that being sorry was the right thing to do! Strangely enough, though Rebecca Mary's view of the matter never occurred to Aunt Olivia, she came by and by to being sorry on her own account. Perhaps she had been all along, underneath her disquietude for Rebecca Mary's sorrow. Perhaps when she thought how quiet it had grown mornings, and what a good chance there was now for a supplementary nap, she was being sorry. When she remembered that she need not buy wheat now and yellow corn, and that the cookies would last longer - perhaps then she was sorry. But she did not know it. It seemed to come upon her with the nature of a surprise on one especial day. She had been working her un-"scrached," untrampled flower-beds.

"My grief!" she ejaculated, suddenly, as if just aware of it. "I declare I believe I miss him, too! I believe to my soul I'd like to hear him crow - I wouldn't mind if he came strutting in here!" And "in here" was Aunt Olivia's beloved garden of flowers. Surely she was being sorry now!

It was the next day that Rebecca Mary's bitterness was sweetened - that she began to be cured. She and the little, white cat went down together to Thomas Jefferson's resting place. When they went home - and they went soon - Rebecca Mary got her diary and began to write in it with eager haste. Her sombre little face had lighted up with some inner gladness, like relief:

"Shes been there and put some lavvender on and pinks. I mean Aunt Olivia. And shes the very fondest of her pinks and lavvender. So she must have loved Tomas Jefferson. Shes sorry. Shes sorry. Shes sorry. And Ime so glad."

Rebecca Mary caught up the little, white cat and cried her first tear of joy on its neck. Then she wrote again:

"Now there are two morners instead of one. Two morners seams so mutch lovinger than only one. I know he must feal better. I think he must have been hurt before and so was I. I wish I dass tell Aunt Olivia how glad I am shes sorry."

But she told only the little, white cat. The Plummer mantle of reticence had fallen too heavily on her narrow little shoulders. What she longed to do she did not "dass." But that evening in her little ruffled nightgown she went to Aunt Olivia's room and thanked her for the ruffles.

"They're beautiful," she murmured, in a small agony of shyness. "I think it was very kind of you to ruffle me - I've always wanted to be. Thank you very much." And then she had scurried away on her bare feet to the safe retreat of her own room under the eaves. Aunt Olivia, left behind, was unconsciously relieved at not having to respond. She was glad the child had discovered the ruffles and was pleased. It was a good sign.

"I'll mix up some pancakes in the morning," Aunt Olivia said, complacently. "Pancakes may help along. Rebecca Mary is fond of 'em."

The pinks and the fragrant lavender appeared to have

Annie Hamilton Donnell

established a certain unspoken comradeship between the two "morners" of Thomas Jefferson. Thereafter Rebecca Mary went about comforted, and Aunt Olivia relieved. The little, white cat purred about the skirts of one and the stubbed-out toes of the other in cheerful content.

"Well?" the minister's wife queried, in a moment of social intercourse after church. She and Aunt Olivia walked down the aisle together.

"She's getting over it - or beginning to," nodded Aunt Olivia. "That other rooster didn't work, but I think the little cat is going to. She hugs it."

"Good! But she still mourns Thomas Jef - "

"Of course!" Aunt Olivia interposed, rather crisply. "You couldn't expect her to get over it all in a minute. He was a remarkable rooster."

"She misses him, herself," inwardly smiled the minister's little wife. Whether by virtue of her relationship to the minister or by her own virtue, she had learned to read human nature with a degree of accuracy.

"I looked at myself in the glass tonight," confessed Rebecca Mary's diary, "but it was on acount of the rufles. I think Ime not quite so homebly in rufles. I think Aunt Olivia was kind to rufle me. I should like to ware this night gown in the day time. I wish folks did."

The pencil slipped out of Rebecca Mary's fingers and rolled on the floor, to the undoing of the little, white cat, who had gone to bed in his basket. Rebecca Mary caught him up as he darted after the pencil, and hugged him in an odd little ecstasy. She felt oddly happy.

"You little, white cat!" she cried, muffledly, her face in his thick coat, "you've waited and waited, but I think I'm going to love you now - you needn't wait any more."

The Feel Doll

The minister uttered a suppressed note of warning as solid little steps sounded in the hall. It was he who threw a hasty covering over the doll. The minister's wife sewed on undisturbedly. She did worse than that.

"Come here, Rhoda," she called, "and tell me which you like better, three tucks or five in this petticoat?"

"Five," promptly, upon inspection. Rhoda pulled away the concealing cover and regarded the stolid doll with tilted head. "She's 'nough like my Pharaoh's Daughter to be a blood relation," she remarked. "She's got the Pharaoh complexion."

"Spoken like MY daughter!" laughed the minister. "But I thought new dolls in this house were always surprises. And here's Mrs. Minister making doll petticoats out in the open!"

"This is Rebecca Mary's - I'm dressing a doll for Rebecca Mary, Robert. She's eleven years old and never had a doll! Rhoda's ten and has had - How many dolls have you had, Rhoda?"

"Gracious! Why, Pharaoh's Daughter, an' Caiapha, an' Esther the Beautiful Queen, an' the Children of Israel - five o' them - an' Mrs. Job, an' - "

"Never mind the rest, dear. You hear, Robert? Do you think Rhoda would be alive now if she'd never had a doll?"

The minister pondered the question. "Maybe not, maybe not," he decided; "but possibly the dolls would have been."

"Don't make me smile, Robert. I'm trying to make you cry. If Rebecca Mary were sixty instead of eleven I should dress her a doll."

"Then why not one for Miss Olivia?"

"I may dress her one," undauntedly, "if I find out she never had one in her life."

"She never did." The minister's voice was positive. "And for that reason, dear, aren't you afraid she would not approve of Rebecca Mary's having one? Isn't it rather a delicate mat - "

"Don't, Robert, don't discourage me. It's going to be such a beautiful doll! And you needn't tell me that poor little eleven-year-old woman-child won't hold out her empty arms for it. Robert, you're a minister; would it be wrong to give it to her STRAIGHT?"

"Straight, dear?"

"Yes; without saying anything to her aunt Olivia. Tell me. Rhoda's gone. Say it as - as liberally as you can."

The minister for answer swept doll, petticoat, and minister's wife into his arms, and kissed them all impartially.

Annie Hamilton Donnell

"Think if it were Rhoda," she pleaded.

"And you were 'Aunt Olivia'? You ask me to think such hard things, dear! If I could stop being a minister long enough - "

"Stop?" she laughed; but she knew she meant keep on. With a sigh she burrowed a little deeper in his neck. "Then I'll ask Aunt Olivia first," she said.

She went back to her tucking. Only once more did she mention Rebecca Mary. The once was after she had come downstairs from tucking the children into bed. She stood in the doorway with the look in her face that mothers have after doing things like that. The minister loved that look.

"Robert, nights when I kiss the children - you knew when you married me that I was foolish - I kiss little lone Rebecca Mary, too. I began the day Thomas Jefferson died - I went to the Rebecca-Mary-est window and threw her a kiss. I went tonight. Don't say a word; you knew when you married me."

Aunt Olivia received the resplendent doll in silence. Plummer honesty and Plummer politeness were at variance. Plummer politeness said: "Thank her. For goodness' sake, aren't you going to thank the minister's wife?" But Plummer honesty, grim and yieldless, said, "You can't thank her, because you're not thankful." So Aunt Olivia sat silent, with her resplendent doll across her knees.

"For Rebecca Mary," the minister's wife was saying, in rather a halting way. "I dressed it for her. I thought perhaps she never - "

"She never," said Aunt Olivia, briefly. Strange that at that particular instant she should remember a trifling incident in the child's far-off childhood. The incident had to do with a little, white nightgown rolled tightly and pinned together. She had found Rebecca Mary in her little waist and petticoat cuddling it in bed.

"It's a dollie. Please 'sh, Aunt Olivia, or you'll wake her up!" the child had whispered, in an agony. "Oh, you're not agoing to turn her back to a nightgown? Don't unpin her, Aunt Olivia - it will kill her! I'll name her after you if you'll let her stay."

"Get up and take your clothes off." Strange Aunt Olivia should remember at this particular instant; should remember, too, that the pin had been a little rusty and came out hard. Rebecca Mary had slid out of bed obediently, but there had been a look on her little brown face as of one bereaved. She had watched the pin come out, and the nightgown unroll, in stricken silence. When it hung released and limp over Aunt Olivia's arm she had given one little cry:

"She's dead!"

The minister's wife was talking hurriedly. Her voice seemed a good way off; it had the effect of coming nearer and growing louder as Aunt Olivia stepped back across the years.

"Of course you are to do as you think best about giving it to her," the minister's wife said, unwillingly. This came of being a minister's wife! "But I think - I have always thought - that little girls ought - I mean Rhoda ought - to have dolls to cuddle. It seems part of their – her - inheritance." This was hard work! If Miss Olivia would not sit there looking like that - .

"As if I'd done something unkind!" thought the gentle little mother, indignantly. She got up presently and went away. But Aunt Olivia, with the doll hanging unhealthily over her arm, followed her to the door. There was something the Plummer honesty insisted upon Aunt Olivia's saying. She said it reluctantly:

"I think I ought to tell you that I've never believed in dolls. I've always thought they were a waste of time and kept children from learning to do useful things. I've brought Rebecca Mary up according to my best light."

"Worst darkness!" thought the minister's wife, hotly.

"She's never had a doll. I never had one. I got along. I could make butter when I was seven. So perhaps you'd better take the doll - "

"No, no! Please keep it, Miss Olivia, and if you should ever change your mind - I mean perhaps sometime - good-bye. It's a beautiful day, isn't it?"

Aunt Olivia took it up into the guest chamber and laid it in an empty bureau drawer. She closed the drawer hastily. She did not feel as duty-proof as she had once felt, before things had happened - softening things that had pulled at her heartstrings and weakened her. The quilt on the guest chamber bed was one of the things; she would not look at it now. And the sheets under the quilt - and the grave of Thomas Jefferson that she could see from the guest chamber window. Aunt Olivia was terribly beset with the temptation to take the doll out to Rebecca Mary in the garden.

"Are you going to do it?" demanded Duty, confronting her. "Are you going to give up all your convictions now? Rebecca Mary's in her twelfth year-pretty late to begin to humor her. I thought you didn't believe in humoring."

"I unpinned the nightgown," parried Aunt Olivia, on the defensive. "I never let her make another one."

"But you're weakening now. You want to let her have THIS doll."

"It seems like part of - of her inheritance."

"Lock that drawer!"

Aunt Olivia turned the key unhappily. It was not that her "convictions" had changed - it was her heart.

She went up at odd times and looked at the doll the minister's wife had dressed. She had an unaccountable, uncomfortable feeling that it was lying there in its coffin - that Rebecca Mary would have said, "She's dead."

It was a handsome doll. Aunt Olivia was not acquainted with dolls, but she acknowledged that. She admired it unwillingly. She liked its clothes - the minister's wife had not spared any pains. She had not stinted in tucks nor ruffles.

Once Aunt Olivia took it out and turned it over in her hands with critical intent, but there was nothing to criticise. It was a beautiful doll. She held it with a curious, shy tenderness. But that time she did not sit down with it. It was the next time.

Annie Hamilton Donnell

The rocker was so near the bureau, and Aunt Olivia was tired - and the doll was already in her arms. She only sat down. For a minute she sat quite straight and unrelaxed, then she settled back a little - a little more. The doll lay heavily against her, its flaxen head touching her breast. After the manner of high-bred dolls, its eyes drooped sleepily.

Aunt Olivia began to rock - a gentle sway back and forth. She was sixty, but this was the first time she had ever rocked a chi - a doll. So she rocked for a little, scarcely knowing it. When she found out, a wave of soft pink dyed her face and flowed upward redly to her hair.

"Well!" Duty jibed, mocking her.

"Don't say a word!" cried poor Aunt Olivia. "I'll put her right back."

"What good will that do?"

"I'll lock her in."

"You've locked her in before."

"I'll - I'll hide the key."

"Where you can find it! Think again."

Aunt Olivia thrust the doll back into its coffin with unsteady hands. The red in her face had faded to a faint, abiding pink. She locked the drawer and drew out the key. She strode to the window and flung it out with a wide sweep of her arm.

The minister's wife, ignorant of the results of her kind little experiment, resolved to question Rebecca Mary the next time she came on an errand. She would do it with extreme caution.

"I'll just feel round," she said. "I want to know if her aunt's given it to her. You think she must have, don't you, Robert? By this time? Why, it was six weeks ago I carried it over! It was such a nice, friendly little doll! By this time they would be such friends - if her aunt gave it to her. Robert, you think - "

"I think it's going to rain," the minister said. But he kissed her to make it easier.

Rebecca Mary came over to bring Aunt Olivia's rule for parson-cake that the minister's wife had asked for.

"Come in, Rebecca Mary," the minister's wife said, cordially. "Don't you want to see the new dress Rhoda's doll is going to have? I suppose you could make your doll's dress yourself?" It seemed a hard thing to say. Feeling round was not pleasant.

"P'haps I could, but she doesn't wear dresses," Rebecca Mary answered, gravely.

"No?" This was puzzling. "Her clothes don't come off, I suppose?" Then it could not be the nice, friendly doll.

"No'm. Nor they don't go on, either. She isn't a feel doll."

"A - what kind did you say, dear?" The minister's wife paused in her work interestedly. Distinctly, Miss Olivia had not given her THE doll; but this doll - "I don't think I quite understood, Rebecca Mary."

"No'm; it's a little hard. She isn't a FEEL doll, I said. I never had a feel one. Mine hasn't any body, just a soul. But she's a great comfort."

"Robert," appealed the minister's wife, helplessly. This was a case for the minister - a case of souls.

"Tell us some more about her, Rebecca Mary," the minister urged, gently. But there was helplessness, too, in his eyes.

"Why, that's all!" returned Rebecca Mary, in surprise. "Of course I can't dress her or undress her or take her out calling. But it's a great comfort to rock her soul to sleep."

"Call Rhoda," murmured the wife to the minister; but Rhoda was already there. She volunteered prompt explanation. There was no hesitation in Rhoda's face.

"She means a make believe doll. Don't you, Rebecca Mary?"

"Yes," Rebecca Mary assented; "that's her other name, I suppose, but I never called her by it."

"What did you call her?" demanded practical Rhoda. "What's her name mean?"

"Rhoda!" - hastily, from the minister's wife. This seemed like sacrilege. But Rhoda's clear, blue eyes were fixed upon Rebecca Mary; she had not heard her mother's warning little word.

A shy color spread thinly over the lean little face of Rebecca Mary. For the space of a breath or two she hesitated.

"Her name's - Felicia," then, softly.

"Robert" - the children had gone out together; the minister's wife's eyes were unashamedly wet - " Robert, I wish you were a - a sheriff instead of a minister. Because I think I would make a better sheriff's wife. Do you know what I would make you do?"

The minister could guess.

"I'd make you ARREST that woman, Robert!"

"Felicia!" But she saw willingness to be a sheriff come into his own eyes and stop there briefly.

"Don't call me 'Felicia' while I feel as wicked as this! Oh, Robert, to think she named her little soul-doll after me!"

"It's a beautiful name."

Suddenly the wickedness was over. She laughed unsteadily.

"It wouldn't be a good name for a sheriff's wife, would it?" she said. "So I'll stay by my own minister."

One day close upon this time Aunt Olivia came abruptly upon Rebecca Mary in the grape arbor. She was sitting in her little rocking chair, swaying back and forth slowly. She did not see Aunt Olivia. What was she was crooning half under her breath?

> "Oh, hush, oh, hush, my dollie;
> Don't worry any more,
> For Rebecca Mary 'n' the angels
> Are watching o'er,
> - O'er 'n' o'er 'n' o'er."

The same words over and over - growing perhaps a little softer and tenderer. Rebecca Mary's arm was crooked as though a little flaxen head lay in the bend of it. Rebecca Mary's brooding little face was gazing downward intently at her empty arm. Quite suddenly it came upon Aunt Olivia that she had seen the child rocking like this before - that she must have seen her often.

> "Rebecca Mary 'n' the angels
> Are watching o'er,"

sang on the crooning little voice in Aunt Olivia's ears.

The doll in its coffin upstairs; down here Rebecca Mary rocking her empty arms. The two thoughts flashed into Aunt Olivia's mind and welded into one. All her vacillations and Duty's sharp reminders occurred to her clearly. She had thought that at last she was proof against temptation, but she had not thought of this. She was not prepared for Rebecca Mary, here in her little rocking chair, rocking her little soul-doll to sleep.

The angels were used to watching o'er, but Aunt Olivia could not bear it. She went away with a strange, unaccustomed ache in her throat. The minister's wife would not have wanted her arrested then.

Aunt Olivia tiptoed away as though Rebecca Mary had said, "'Sh!" She was remembering, as she went, the brief, sweet moment when she had sat like that and rocked, with the doll the minister's wife dressed, in her arms. It seemed to establish a new link of kinship between her and Rebecca Mary.

She ran plump into Duty.

"Oh!" she gasped. She was a little stunned. Aunt Olivia's Duty was solid.

"I know where you've been. I tried get there in time."

"You're too late," Aunt Olivia said, firmly, "Don't stop me; there's something I must do before it gets too dark. It's six o'clock now."

"Wait!" commanded Duty. "Are you crazy? You don't mean - "

"Go back there and look at that child - and hear what she's singing! Stay long enough to take it all in - don't hurry."

But Duty barred her way, grim and stern.

Palely she put up both her hands and thrust it aside. She did not once look back at it.

Already it was dusky under the guest chamber window. She had to stoop and peer and feel in the long tangle of grass. She kept on patiently with the Plummer kind of patience that never gave up. She was eager and smiling, as though something pleasant

Annie Hamilton Donnell

were at the end of the peering and stooping and feeling.

Aunt Olivia was hunting for a key.

The Plummer Kind

The doll's name was Olivicia.

Rebecca Mary had evolved the name from her inner consciousness and her intense gratitude to Aunt Olivia and the minister's wife. She had put Aunt Olivia first with instinctive loyalty, though in the secret little closet of her soul she had longed to call the beautiful being Felicia, intact and sweet. She did not know the meaning of Felicia, but she knew that the doll, as it lay in the loving cradle of her arms, gazing upward with changeless placidity and graciousness, looked as one should look whose name was Felicia. Greater compliment than this Rebecca Mary could not have paid the minister's wife.

"Olivicia," she had placed the being on the sill of the attic window, stood confronting, addressing it: "Olivicia, it's coming - it is very near to! Sit there and listen and smile - oh yes, smile, SMILE. I don't wonder! I would too, only I'm too glad. When you're TOO glad you can't smile. I've been waiting for it to come. Olivicia, seems as if I'd been waiting a thousan' years. You're so young, you've only lived such little while, of course I don't expect you understand the deep-downness inside o' me when I think - "

The address fluttered and came to a standstill here.

Annie Hamilton Donnell

Rebecca Mary was suddenly minded that Olivicia was in the dark; must be enlightened before she could smile understandingly.

"Why, you poor dear! - why, you don't know what it is that's coming and that's near to! It's the - city, Olivicia," enlightened Rebecca Mary, gently, to insure against shock. "Aunt Olivia's going - to - the - city."

In Rebecca Mary's dreamings it had always been THE city. It did not need local habitation and a name; enough that it had streets upon streets, houses upon houses upon houses, a dazzling swirl of men, women, and little children - noise, glitter, glory. In her dreamings the city was something so wondrous and grand that Heaven might have been its name. The streets upon streets were not paved with gold, of course - of course she knew they were not paved with gold! But in spite of herself she knew that she would be disappointed if they did not shine.

Aunt Olivia had said it that morning. At breakfast - quite matter-of-factly. Think of saying it matter-of-factly!

"I'm going to the city soon, Rebecca Mary," she had said, between sips of her tea. "Perhaps by Friday week, but I haven't set the day, really. There's a good deal to do."

Rebecca Mary had been helping do it all day. Now it was nearly time for the pageant of red and gold in the west that Rebecca Mary loved, and she had come up here with the beautiful being to watch it through the tiny panes of the attic window, but more to ease the aching rapture in her soul by speech. She must say it out loud. The city - the city - to the city of streets and houses and men and wonders upon wonders!

Olivicia had come in the capacity of calm listener; for nothing excited Olivicia.

"I," Aunt Olivia had said, but Aunt Olivia usually said "I." There was no discouragement in that to Rebecca Mary. It did not for a moment occur to her that "I" did not mean "we."

The valise they had got down from its cobwebby niche was roomy; it would hold enough for two. Rebecca Mary knew that, because she had packed it so many times in her dreamings. She wished Aunt Olivia would let her pack it now. She knew just where she would put everything - her best dress and Aunt Olivia's (for of course they would wear their second-bests), their best hats and shoes and gloves. Their nightgowns she would roll tightly and put in one end, for it doesn't hurt nightgowns to be rolled tightly. Of course she would not put anything heavy, like hair brushes and shoes and things, on top of anything - unless it was the nightgowns, for it doesn't hurt -

"Oh, Olivicia - oh, Olivicia, how I hope she'll say, 'Rebecca Mary, you may pack the valise'! I could do it with my eyes shut, I've done it so many, many times!"

But Aunt Olivia did not say it. One day and then another went by without her saying it, and then one morning Rebecca Mary knew by the plump, well-fed aspect of the valise that it was packed. Aunt Olivia had packed it in the night.

There was no one else in the room when Rebecca

Annie Hamilton Donnell

Mary made her disappointing little discovery. She went over to the plump valise and prodded it gently with her finger. But it is so difficult to tell in that way whether your own best dress, your own best hat, best shoes, best gloves, are in there. Rebecca Mary hurried upstairs and looked in her closet and in her "best" bureau drawer.

They were not there! In her relief she caught up the beautiful being and strained her hard, lifeless little body to her own warm breast. If she had not been Rebecca Mary, she would have danced about the room.

"Oh, I'm so relieved, Olivicia!" she laughed, softly. "If they're not up here, THEY'RE DOWN THERE. They've got to be somewhere. They're in that valise - valise - vali-i-ise!"

Rebecca Mary had never been to a city, and within her remembrance Aunt Olivia had never been. Curiosity was not a Plummer trait, hence Rebecca Mary had never asked many questions about the remote period before her own advent into Aunt Olivia's life. The same Plummer restraint kept her now from asking questions. There was nothing to do but wait, but the waiting was illumined by her joyous anticipations.

Oddly enough, Aunt Olivia seemed to have no anticipations - at least joyous ones. Her, thin, grave face may even have looked a little thinner and graver, IF Rebecca Mary had thought to notice."

The night the lean old valise took on plumpness, Aunt Olivia went often into Mary's little room. Many of the times she came out very shortly with the child's "best" things trailing from her arms, but once or twice she stayed rather long - long enough to stand beside a little white bed and look down on a flushed little face. A pair of wide-open eyes watched her smilingly from the pillows, but they were not Rebecca Mary's eyes, and Olivicia was altogether trustworthy.

An odd thing happened - but Olivicia never told. Why should she publish abroad that she had lain there and seen Aunt Olivia bend once - bend twice - over Rebecca Mary and kiss her?

Softly, patiently, very wearily, Aunt Olivia went in and out. The things she brought out in her arms she folded carefully and packed, but not in the lank old valise. She put them all with tender painstaking into a quaint little carpetbag. When the work was done she set the bag away out of sight, and went about packing her own things in the old valise.

The day before, she had been to see the minister and the minister's wife. She called for them both, and sat down gravely and made her proposition. It was startling only because of the few words it took to make it. Otherwise it was very pleasant, and the minister and the minister's wife received it with nods and smiles.

"Of course, Miss Olivia - why, certainly!" smiled and nodded the minister.

"Why, it will be delightful - and Rhoda will be so pleased!" nodded and smiled the minister's wife. But after their caller had gone she faced the minister with indignant eyes.

"Why did you let her?" she demanded. "Why did you spoil it all by that?"

Annie Hamilton Donnell

"Because she was Miss Olivia," he answered, gently.

"Yes - yes, I suppose so," reluctantly; "but, anyway, you needn't have let her do it in advance. Actually it made me blush, Robert!"

The minister rubbed his cheeks tentatively. "Made me, too," he admitted, "but I respect Miss Olivia so much - "

The minister's wife tacked abruptly to her other source of indignation.

"Why doesn't she TAKE Rebecca Mary? Robert, wait! You know it isn't because - You know better!"

"It isn't because, dear - I know better," he hurried, assuringly. The minister was used to her little indignations and loved them for being hers. They were harmless, too, and wont to have a good excuse for being. This one, now - the minister in his heart wondered that Miss Olivia did not take Rebecca Mary.

"It would be such a treat. Robert, you think what a treat it would be to Rebecca Mary!"

"Still, dear - "

"I don't want to be still! I want Rebecca Mary to have that treat!" But she kissed him in token of being willing to drop it there - it was her usual token - and ran away to get a little room ready. There was not a device known to the minister's wife that she did not use to make that room pleasant.

"Shall I take your pincushion, Rhoda?" Rhoda had

come up to help.

"Yes," eagerly, "and I'll write Welcome with the pins."

"And the little fan to put on the wall - the pink one?"

"Yes, yes; let me spread it out, mamma!"

"That's grand. Now if we only had a pink quilt - "

"I 'only have' one!" laughed Rhoda, hurrying after it.

The whole little room when they left, like the pins in the pincushion, spelled "WELCOME."

Aunt Olivia got up earlier than usual one day and went about the house for a survey. The valise and the little carpetbag she carried downstairs and out on to the front steps. Her face was whitened as if by a long night's vigil. When she called Rebecca Mary it was with a voice strained hoarse. The beautiful being Olivicia watched her with intent, unwinking gaze. Could it be Olivicia understood?

"Hurry and dress, Rebecca Mary; there's a good deal to do," Aunt Olivia said at the door. She did not go in. "Yes, in your second-best - don't you see I've put it out. You can wear that every day now, till - for a while." Something in the voice startled Rebecca Mary out of her subdued ecstasy and sent her down to breakfast with a nameless fear tugging at her heart.

"You're going to stay at the minister's - I've paid your board in advance," Aunt Olivia said, monotonously, as if it were her lesson. She did not look at Rebecca Mary. "I've put in your long-sleeve aprons so you can

Annie Hamilton Donnell

help do up the dishes. There's plenty of handkerchiefs to last. You mustn't forget your rubbers when it's wet, or to make up your bed yourself. I don't want you to make the minister's wife any more trouble than you can help."

The lesson went monotonously on, but Rebecca Mary scarcely heard. She had heard the first sentence - her sentence, poor child! "You're going to stay at the minister's - stay at the minister's - stay at the minister's." It said itself over and over again in her ears. In her need for somebody to lean on, her startled gaze sought the beautiful being across the room in agonized appeal.

But Olivicia was staring smilingly at Aunt Olivia. ET TU, OLIVICIA!

If Rebecca Mary had noticed, there was an appealing, wistful look in Aunt Olivia's eyes too, in odd contrast to the firm lips that moved steadily on with their lesson:

"You can walk to school with Rhoda, you'll enjoy that. You've never had folks to walk with. And you can stay with her, only you mustn't forget your stents. I've put in some towels to hem. Maybe the minister's wife has got something; if so, hem hers first. You'll be like one o' the family, and they're nice folks, but I want you to keep right on being a Plummer."

Years afterwards Rebecca Mary remembered the dizzy dance of the bottles in the caster - they seemed to join hands and sway and swing about their silver circlet and how Aunt Olivia's buttons marched and counter-marched up and down Aunt Olivia's alpaca dress. She did not look above the buttons - she did not dare to. If she was to keep right on being a Plummer, she must not cry.

"That's all," she heard through the daze and dizziness, "except that I can't tell when I'll be back. It - ain't decided. Likely I shan't be able - there won't be much chance to write, and you needn't expect me to. No need to write me either. That's all, I guess."

The stage that came for Aunt Olivia dropped the little carpetbag and Rebecca Mary at the minister's. In the brief interval between the start and the dropping, Rebecca Mary sat, stiff and numb, on the edge of the high seat and gazed out unfamiliarly at the familiar landmarks they lurched past. At any other time the knowledge that she was going to the minister's to stay - to live - would have filled her with staid joy. At any other time - but THIS time only a dull ache filled her little dreary world. Everything seemed to ache - the munching cows in the Trumbull pasture, the cats on the doorsteps, the dog loping along beside the stage, the stage driver's stooping old back. Aunt Olivia was going to the city - Rebecca Mary wasn't going to the city. There was no room in the world for anything but that and the ache.

Rebecca Mary's indignation was not born till night. Then, lying in the dainty bed under Rhoda's pink quilt, her mood changed. Until then she had only been disappointed. But then she sat up suddenly and said bitter things about Aunt Olivia.

"She's gone to have a good time all to herself - and she might have taken me. She didn't, she didn't, and she might've. She wanted all the good time herself! She

Annie Hamilton Donnell

didn't want me to have any!"

"Rebecca Mary! - did you speak, dear?" It was the gentle voice of the minister's wife outside the door. Rebecca Mary's red little hands unwrung and dropped on the pink quilt.

"No'm, I did - I mean yes'm, I didn't - I mean - "

"You don't feel sick? There isn't anything the matter, dear?"

"No'm - oh, yes'm, yes'm!" for there was something the matter. It was Aunt Olivia. But she must not say it - must not cry - must keep right on being a Plummer.

"Robert, I didn't go in - I couldn't," the minister's wife said, back in the cheery sitting room. "I suppose you think I'd have gone in and comforted her, taken her right in my arms and comforted her the Rhoda way, but I didn't."

"No?" The minister's voice was a little vague on account of the sermon on his knees.

"I seemed to know - something told me right through that door - that she'd rather I wouldn't. Robert, if the child is homesick, it's a different kind of homesickness."

"The Plummer kind," he suggested. The minister was coming to.

"Yes, the Plummer kind, I suppose, Plummers are such - such PLUMMERY persons, Robert!"

Upstairs under the pink quilt the rigid little figure relaxed just enough to admit of getting out of bed and fumbling in the little carpetbag. With her diary in her hand - for Aunt Olivia had remembered her diary - Rebecca Mary went to the window and sat down. She had to hold the cookbook up at a painful angle and peer at it sharply, for the moonlight that filtered into the little room through the vines was dim and soft.

"Aunt Olivia has gone to the city and I haven't," painfully traced Rebecca Mary. "She wanted the good time all to herself. I shall never forgive Aunt Olivia the Lord have mercy on her." Then Rebecca Mary went back to bed. She dreamed that the cars ran off the track and they brought Aunt Olivia's pieces home to her. In the dreadful dream she forgave Aunt Olivia.

It was very pleasant at the minister's and the minister's wife's. Rebecca Mary felt the warmth and pleasantness of it in every fibre of her body and soul. But she was not happy nor warm. She thought it was indignation against Aunt Olivia - she did not know she was homesick. She did not know why she went to the old home every day after school and wandered through Aunt Olivia's flower garden, and sat with little brown chin palm-deep on the doorsteps. Gradually the indignation melted out of existence and only the homesickness was left. It sat on her small, lean face like a little spectre. It troubled the minister's wife.

"What can we do, Robert?" she asked.

"What?" he echoed; for the minister, too, was troubled.

"She wanders about like a little lost soul. When she

Annie Hamilton Donnell

plays with the children it's only the outside of her that plays."

"Only the outside," he nodded.

"Last night I went in, Robert, and - and tried the Rhoda way. I think she liked it, but it didn't comfort her. I am sure now that it is homesickness, Robert." They were both sure, but the grim little spectre sat on, undaunted by all their kindnesses.

"When thy father and thy mother forsake the," wrote Rebecca Mary in the cookbook diary, "and thy Aunt Olivia for I know it means and thy Aunt Olivia then the Lord will take the up, but I dont feal as if anyboddy had taken me up. The ministers wife did once but of course she had to put me down again rite away. She is a beutiful person and I love her but she is differunt from thy father and thy mother and thy Aunt Olivia. Ide rather have Aunt Olivia take me up than to have the Lord."

It was when she shut the battered little book this time that Rebecca Mary remembered one or two things that had happened the morning Aunt Olivia went away. It was queer how she HADN'T remembered them before.

She remembered that Aunt Olivia had taken her sharp little face between her own hands and looked down wistfully at it - wistfully, Rebecca Mary remembered now, though she did not call it by that name. She remembered Aunt Olivia had said, "You needn't hem anything unless it's for the minister's wife - never mind the towels I put in." That was almost the last thing she had said. She had put her head out of the stage door to say it. Rebecca Mary had hemmed a towel each day.

There were but two left, and she resolved to hem both of those tomorrow. A sudden little longing was born within her for more towels to hem for Aunt Olivia.

It was nearly three weeks after Rebecca Mary's entrance into the minister's family when the letter came. It was directed to Rebecca Mary, and lay on her plate when she came home from school.

"Oh, look, you've got a letter, Rebecca Mary!" heralded Rhoda, joyfully. Then her face fell, for maybe the letter would say Aunt Olivia was coming home.

"Is it from your aunt Olivia?" she asked, anxiously.

"No," Rebecca Mary said, in slow surprise. "The writing isn't, anyway, and the name is another one - "

"Oh! Oh! Maybe she's got mar - "

"Rhoda!" cautioned the minister.

This is the letter Rebecca Mary read:

"Dear Rebecca Mary, - You see I know your name from your aunt. She talked about you all the time, but I am writing you of my own accord. She does not know it. I think you will like to know that at last we are feeling very hopeful about your aunt. We have been very anxious since the operation, she had so little strength to rally with. But now if she keeps on as well as this you will have her home again in a little while. The doctors say three weeks. She is the patientest patient in the ward.

Yours very truly,

Annie Hamilton Donnell

Sara Ellen Nesbitt, Nurse"
Ward A, Emmons Hospital

That was the letter. Rebecca Mary's face grew a little whiter at every line of it. At every line understanding grew clearer, till at the end she knew it all. She gave a little cry, and ran out of the room. Love and remorse and sympathy fought for first place in her laboring little breast. In the next few minutes she lived so long a time and thought so many thoughts! But above everything else towered joy that Aunt Olivia was coming home. Rebecca Mary's eyes blazed with pride at being a Plummer. This kind of courage was the Plummer kind. The child's lank little figure seemed to grow taller and straighter. She held up her head splendidly and exulted. She felt like going up on the minister's housetop and proclaiming: "She's my aunt Olivia! She's mine! She's mine - I'm a Plummer, too! All o' you listen, she's my aunt Olivia, and she's coming home!"

Suddenly the child flung out her arms towards the south where Aunt Olivia was. And though she stood quite still, something within her seemed to spring away and go hurrying through the clear air.

"I shouldn't suppose Aunt Olivia would ever forgive me, but she's Aunt Olivia and she will," wrote Rebecca Mary that night, her small, dark face full of a solemn peace - it seemed so long since she had been full of peace before. She wrote on eagerly:

"When she gets home Ime going to hug her I can't help it if it wont be keeping right on."

Rebecca Mary measured them. Against the woodshed wall, with chalk - it was not altogether an easy thing to do. The result startled her. With rather unsteady little fingers she measured from chalk mark to floor again, to make sure it was as bad as that. It was even a little worse.

"Oh," sighed Rebecca Mary, "to think they belong to me - to think they're hitched on!" She gazed down at them with scorn and was ashamed of them. She tried to conceal their length with her brief skirts; but when she straightened up, there they were again, as long as ever. She sat down suddenly on the shed floor and drew them up underneath her. That was temporarily a relief. "If I sit here world without end nobody'll see 'em," grimly smiled Rebecca Mary.

It was her legs Rebecca Mary measured against the woodshed wall. It was her legs she was ashamed of. No wonder the minister's wife had said to the minister going home from meeting, with Rebecca Mary behind them unawares, - no wonder she had said, "Robert, HAVE you noticed Rebecca Mary's legs?"

Rebecca Mary had not heard the reply of the minister, for of course she had gone away then. If she had stayed she would have heard him say, with exaggerated prudery, "Felicia! My dear! Were you alluding to Rebecca Mary's limbs?" for the minister wickedly remembered inadvertent occasions when he himself had called legs legs.

"LEGS," the minister's wife repeated, calmly - "Rebecca Mary's are too long for limbs. Robert, that child will grow up one of these days!"

"They all do," sighed the minister. "It's human nature, dear. You'll be telling me next that there's something the matter with Rhoda's - legs."

The minister's wife gazed thoughtfully ahead at a little trio fast approaching the vanishing point. Her eyes grew a little wistful.

"There is now, perhaps, but I haven't noticed - I won't look!" she murmured. "And, anyway, Robert, Rhoda will give us a little time to get used to it in. But Rebecca Mary isn't the Rhoda kind - I don't believe Rebecca Mary will give us even three days of grace!"

"I always supposed Rebecca Mary was born that way - grown up," the minister remarked, tucking a gloved hand comfortably close under his arm. "I wouldn't let it worry me, dear."

"Oh, I don't - not worry, really," she said, smiling - "only her legs startled me a little today. If she were mine, I should let her dresses down."

"If she were Rhod - "

"She isn't, she's Rebecca Mary. Probably if I were Miss Olivia I would let Rhoda's down!" And she knew she would.

Rebecca Mary on the woodshed floor sat and thought "deep-down" thoughts. Her eyes were fixed dreamily on a big knothole before her, and the thoughts seemed to come out of it and stand before her, demanding imperiously to be thought. One after another - a relentless procession.

"Think me," the first one had commanded. "I'm the Thought of Growing Up. I saw you measuring your legs, and I concluded it was time for me to introduce myself. I had to come some time, didn't I?"

"Oh yes," breathed Rebecca Mary, sadly. "I don't suppose I could expect you to stay in there always; but - but I'm not very glad to see you. You needn't have come so SUDDEN," she added, with gentle resentment.

The Thought of Growing Up crept into her mind and nestled down there. As thoughts go, it was not an unkind one.

"You'll get used to me sometime and like me," it said, comfortingly. But Rebecca Mary knew better. She drove it out.

Why must legs keep on growing and unwelcome Thoughts come out of knotholes? Why could not little girls keep on sewing stents and learning arithmetic and carrying beautiful doll-beings to bed? Why had the Lord created little girls like this - this growing kind?

"If I had made the world," began Rebecca Mary - but stopped in a hurry. The irreverence of presuming to make a better world than the Lord shamed her.

"I suppose He knew best, but if He'd ever been a little girl - " This was worse than the other. Rebecca Mary hastily dismissed the world and its Maker from her musings for fear of further irreverences.

One Thought came out of the knothole, illustrated. It was leading a tall woman-girl by the hand - no, it was pushing it as though the woman-girl were loath to come.

"Come along," urged the new Thought, laughingly. "Here she is - this is Rebecca Mary. Rebecca Mary, this is YOU! You needn't be afraid of each other, you two. Take a good long look and get acquainted."

The woman-girl was tall and straight. She had Rebecca Mary's hair, Rebecca Mary's eyes, mouth, little pointed chin. But not Rebecca Mary's legs - unless the long skirts covered them. She was rather comely and pleasant to look at. But Rebecca Mary tried not to look.

"She's got a lover - -some day she'll be getting married," the new Thought said more abruptly, startlingly, than grammatically. And then with a little muffled cry Rebecca Mary put out her hands and pushed the woman-girl away - back into the knothole whence she had come. The Thought, too, for she had no room in her mind for thoughts like that.

"My aunt Olivia wouldn't allow me to think of you," she explained in dismissing them. "And," with dignity she added, "neither would Rebecca Mary."

It was to be as the minister's wife had prophesied - there were to be not even the three days of grace allowed by law when Rebecca Mary grew up. Sitting there with her legs, her poor little unappreciated legs, the innocent cause of the whole trouble, curled out of sight, Rebecca Mary planned that there should be but one day of grace. She would allow one day more to be a little girl in, and then she would grow up. But that one day - Rebecca Mary got up hastily and went to find Aunt Olivia.

"Aunt Olivia," she began, without preamble - Rebecca Mary never preambled - "Aunt Olivia, may I have a holiday tomorrow?"

Aunt Olivia was rocking in her easy chair on the porch. It had taken her sixty-two years to learn to sit in an easy chair and rock. Even now, and she had been home from the hospital many months, she felt a little as though the friendly birds that perched on the porch railing were twittering tauntingly, "Plummer! Plummer! Plummer! - rocking in an easy chair!"

"May I, Aunt Olivia?" It was an unusual occurrence for Rebecca Mary to ask again so soon. But this was an unusual occurrence. Aunt Olivia's thin face turned affectionately towards the child.

"School doesn't begin again tomorrow, does it?" she said in surprise. Weren't all Rebecca Mary's days now holidays?

"Oh no - -no'm. But I mean may I skip my stents? And - and may I soak the kettles and pans? Just tomorrow."

"Just tomorrow," repeated bewildered Aunt Olivia - "

Annie Hamilton Donnell

soak your - stents - "

"Because it's going to be a pretty busy day. It's going to be a - a celebration," Rebecca Mary said, softly. There was a strangely exalted look on her face. Oddly enough she was not afraid that Aunt Olivia would say no.

Aunt Olivia said yes. She did not ask any questions about the celebration, on account of the exalted look. She could wait. But the bewildered look stayed for a while on her thin face. Rebecca Mary was a queer child, a queer child - but she was a dear child. Dearness atoned for queerness in Aunt Olivia's creed.

The celebration began early the next morning before Aunt Olivia was up. She lay in bed and heard it begin. Rebecca Mary out in the dewy garden was singing at the top of her voice. Aunt Olivia had never heard her sing like that before - not at the top. Her sweet, shrill voice sounded rather unacquainted with such free heights as that, and the woman in the bed wondered with a staid little smile if it did not make Rebecca Mary feel as she felt when she sat in the easy chair rocking.

Rebecca Mary sang hymns mostly, but interspersed in her programme were bits of Mother Goose set to original tunes - she had learned the Mother Goose of the minister's Littlest Little Boy - and original bits set to familiar tunes. It was a wild little orgy of song.

"My grief!" Aunt Olivia ejaculated under her breath; but she did not mean her grief. Other people might think Rebecca Mary was crazy - not Aunt Olivia. But yet she wondered a little and found it hard to wait.

Rebecca Mary washed the breakfast cup and plates, but put the pans and kettles to soak, and hurried away to her play. There was so much playing to be done before the sun set on her opportunity. She had made a little programme on a slip of paper, with approximate times allotted to each item. As:

Tree climbing...1 hr.
(Do not tare anything)
Mud pies ...1 hr. and 1/2.
(Do not get anything muddy)
Tea party...2 hrs.
(Do not break anything)
Skipping...1/2 hr.

Rebecca Mary had written 1 hr. at first opposite skipping, but it had rather appalled her to think of skipping for so long a period of time, and, with a sense of being already out of breath, she had hurriedly erased the 1 and substituted 1/2. Underneath she had written, (" Do not tip over anything"). All the items had cautionary parentheses underneath them, for Rebecca Mary did not wish the celebration to injure "anything." Not this last day, when all the days of all the years before it, that had gone to make up her little girlhood, nothing had been torn or muddied or tipped over.

Rebecca Mary had never climbed trees, had never made mud pies, never had tea parties, nor skipped. It was with rather a hesitating step that she went forward to meet them all. She was even a little awed. But she went. No item on her programme was omitted.

From her rocker on the porch Aunt Olivia watched proceedings with quiet patience. It was a good vantage point - she could see nearly all of the celebration. The

Annie Hamilton Donnell

tree Rebecca Mary climbed was on the edge of the old orchard next to Aunt Olivia, and there was a providential little rift through the shrubbery and vines that intervened. This part of the programme she could see almost too clearly, for it must be confessed that this part startled Aunt Olivia out of her calm. It - it was so unexpected. She stopped rocking and leaned forward in her chair to peer more sharply. What was the child - "She's climbing a tree!" breathed Aunt Olivia in undisguised astonishment. Even as she breathed it, there came to her faintly the snapping of twigs and flutter of leaves. Then all was quite still, but she could discern with her pair of trusty Plummer eyes two long legs gently dangling.

If Aunt Olivia had known, Rebecca Mary, too, was startled. It - it was so strange an experience. She was not in the least afraid - it was a mental start rather than a physical one. When she had reached the limb set down in her programme she sat on it in a little daze of bewildered delight. She liked it!

"Why, why, it's nice!" Rebecca Mary breathed. Her turn had come for undisguised astonishment. The leaves all about her nodded to her and stroked her cheeks and hair and hands. They whispered things into her ears. They were such friendly little leaves!

Nothing looked quite the same up there. It was a little as if she were in a new world, and she felt odd thrills of pride, as probably people who had discovered countries and rivers and north poles felt. Through a rift in the leaves she could see with her good Plummer eyes a swaying spot of brown and white that was Aunt Olivia rocking. Suddenly Rebecca Mary experienced a pang of remorse that she had wasted so many opportunities like this - that this was her only one. She wished she had put 2 hrs. instead of 1 hr. over against "Tree climbing," but it was too late now. She had borrowed Aunt Olivia's open-faced gold watch to serve as timekeeper, and promptly at the expiration of the 1 hr. she slid down through the crackling twigs and friendly leaves to the old world below. She did not allow herself to look back, but she could not help the sigh. It was going to be harder to grow up than she had thought it would be.

The mud pies she made with conscientious care as Rhoda, the minister's little girl, had said she used to make them. She made rows and rows of them and set them in the sun to bake. There were raisin stones in them all and crimped edges around them . It did not take nearly all the 1 hr. and 1/2, so she made another and still another batch. When the time was up she did not sigh, but she had had rather a good time. How many mud pies she HADN'T made in all those years that were to end today!

Olivicia and the little white cat went to the tea party. Rebecca Mary thought of inviting Aunt Olivia - she got as far as the porch steps, but no farther. She caught a glimpse of her own legs and shrank back sensitively. They seemed to have grown since she measured them against the woodshed wall. Rebecca Mary felt the contrast between her legs and the tea party. Aunt Olivia never knew how near she had come to being invited to take part in the celebration, at Article III. on the programme.

Rhoda had had tea parties unnumbered, like the sands of the sea. She had described them fluently, so Rebecca Mary was not as one in the dark. She knew

Annie Hamilton Donnell

how to cut the bread and the cake into tiny dice, and the cookies into tiny rounds. She knew how to make the cambric tea and to arrange the jelly and flowers. But Rhoda had forgotten to tell her how to make a rose pie - how to select two large rose leaves for upper and under crust, and to fill in the pie between them with pink and white rose petals and sugar in alternate layers. Press until "done." Why had Rhoda forgotten? It seemed a pity that there was no rose pie at Rebecca Mary's tea party - and no time left to make one.

"Will you take sugar in your tea, Olivicia?" Rebecca Mary asked, shyly. She sat on the ground with her legs drawn under her out of sight, but there were little warm spots in her cheeks. She had not expected to be - ashamed. If there had been a knothole anywhere, she thought to herself, the Thought of Growing Up would have come out of it and confronted her and reminded her of her legs.

"Will you help yourself to the bread? Won't you have another cookie?" She left nothing out, and gradually the strangeness wore away. It got gradually to be a good time. "How many tea parties," thought Rebecca Mary, "there might have been!"

Rebecca Mary was skipping, when the minister's wife came to call on Aunt Olivia. It was the minister's wife who discovered it. Aunt Olivia caught the indrawing of her breath and saw her face. Then Aunt Olivia discovered it, and a delicate color overspread her thin cheeks and rose to her temples. Now what was the child -

"Rhoda is a great skipper," the minister's wife said, hurriedly. But it was the wrong thing - she knew it was the wrong thing.

"Rebecca Mary is having a - celebration," hurried Aunt Olivia; but she wished she had not, for it seemed like trying to excuse Rebecca Mary. She, too, had said the wrong thing.

"How pleasant it is out here!" tried again the minister's wife.

"Yes, it's cool," Aunt Olivia agreed, gratefully. After that the things they said were right things. The fantastic little figure down there in the orchard, skipping wildly, determinedly, was in none of them. Both of them felt it to be safer. But the minister's wife's gaze dwelt on the skipping figure and followed it through its amazing mazes, in spite of the minister's wife.

"I couldn't have helped it, Robert," she said. "Not if you'd been there preaching 'Thou shalt not' to me! You would have looked too, while you were preaching. You can't imagine, sitting there at that desk, what the temptation was - Robert, you don't suppose Rebecca Mary has gone crazy?"

"Felicia! You frighten me!"

"No, *I* don't suppose either. But it was certainly very strange. It was almost ALARMING, Robert. And she didn't know how at all. I wanted to go down and show her!"

"It seems to me" - the minister spoke impressively "that it is not Rebecca Mary who has gone crazy - "

Annie Hamilton Donnell

"Why, the idea! Haven't I made it plain?" laughed she. "I'll speak in A B C's then. Rebecca Mary was SKIPPING, Robert - skipping skipping."

"Then it's Rebecca Mary," the minister murmured.

"That's what I'm afraid - didn't I say so? Or else it's her second childhood - "

"First, you mean. If THAT'S it, don't let's say a word, dear - don't breathe, Felicia, for fear we'll stop it."

"Dear child!" the minister's wife said, tenderly. "I wish I'd gone down there and shown her how. And I'd have told her - Robert, I'd have told her how to climb a tree! Don't tell the parish."

The day was to end at sunset, from sunrise to sunset, Rebecca Mary had decreed. The last article on her crumpled little programme was, "Saying Good-by to Olivicia(Don't cry)." It was going to be the most difficult thing of all the articles. Olivicia had existed so short a time comparatively - it might not have been as difficult if there had always been an Olivicia. "Or it might have been harder," Rebecca Mary said. She went towards that article with reluctant feet. But it had to come.

The bureau drawer was all ready. Rebecca Mary had lined it with something white and soft and sweetened it with dried rose petals spiced in the century-old Plummer way. It bore rather grewsome resemblance to Olivicia's coffin, but it was not grewsome to Rebecca Mary. She laid the doll in it with the tender little swinging motion mothers use in laying down their tiny sleepers.

"There, there the-re!" crooned Rebecca Mary, softly, brooding over the beautiful being. "You'll rest there sweetly after your mother is grown up. And you'll try not to miss her, won't you? You'll understand, Olivicia? - oh, Olivicia!" But she did not cry. Her eyes were very bright. For several minutes she stood there stooped over painfully, gazing down into the cof - the bureau drawer, wherein lay peaceful Olivicia. She was saying good-bye in her heart - she never said it aloud.

"Dear," very softly indeed, "you are sure you understand? Everybody has to grow up, dear. It - it hurts, but you have to. I mean I'VE got to. I wouldn't so soon if it wasn't for my legs. But they keep right on growing - they're awful, dear! - I can't stop 'em. Olivicia, lie right there and be thankful you're a doll! But I wish you could open your eyes and look at me just once more."

Rebecca Mary shut the drawer gently. It was over - no, she would say one thing more to the beautiful being in there. She bent to the keyhole.

"Olivicia!" she called in a tender whisper, "I shall be right here nights. We shan't be far away from each other."

But it would not be like lying in each other's arms - oh, not at all like that. Rebecca Mary caught her breath; it was perilously like a sob. Then she girded up her loins and went away to meet her fate - the common fate of all.

She was very tired. The day had been a strain upon her that was beginning now to tell. To put all one's childhood into one day - that is not easy.

Annie Hamilton Donnell

Article VI. was the last. In a way, it was a rest to Rebecca Mary, for it entailed merely a visit to the woodshed. She could sit quietly on the floor opposite the knothole and wait for the Thoughts. If the Thought of Growing Up came out tonight, she would say: "Oh, well, you may stay - you needn't go back. I'm not any glad to see you, but I'm ready. I suppose I shall get used to you."

What Thoughts came out of the knothole to Rebecca Mary she never told to any one. It was nearly dark when she went away, planting her feet firmly, holding her head straight - Rebecca Mary Plummer. She went to find Aunt Olivia and tell her. On the way, she stopped to get Aunt Olivia's shawl, for it was getting chilly out on the porch. Significantly the first thing Rebecca Mary did after she began to grow up was to get the shawl and lay it over Aunt Olivia's spare shoulders. The second thing was to bend to the scant gray hair and lightly rub it with her cheek. It was a Rebecca Mary kiss.

Out in front of the rocking chair, still straight and firm, she told Aunt Olivia.

"It's over - I think I put everything in," she said. "I thought you ought to know, so I came to tell you. I'm ready to grow up."

After all, if Rebecca Mary had known, her "programme" had not ended with Article VI. Here was another. Take the pencil in your steady little fingers, Rebecca Mary, and write:

Article VII. - Growing up. (Do not break Aunt Olivia's heart.)

Un-Plummered

Aunt Olivia sighed. It was the third time since she had begun to let Rebecca Mary down. The third sigh was the longest one. Oh, this letting down of children who would grow up!

"I won't do it!" Aunt Olivia rebelled, fiercely, but she took up her scissors again at Duty's nudge.

"You don't want people laughing at her, do you?" Duty said, sensibly. "Well, then, rip out that hem and face up that skirt and stop sighing. What can't be cured must be endur - "

"I'm ripping it out," Aunt Olivia interrupted, crisply. But Duty was not to be silenced.

"You ought to have done it before," dictatorially. "You've known all along that Rebecca Mary was growing up."

Aunt Olivia, like the proverbial worm, turned.

"I didn't know till Rebecca Mary told me," she retorted; then the rebellion died out of her thin face and tenderness came and took its place. Aunt Olivia was thinking of the time when Rebecca Mary told her. She gazed past Duty, past the skirt across her knees, out

Annie Hamilton Donnell

through the porch vines, and saw Rebecca Mary coming to tell her. She saw the shawl the child was bringing, felt it laid on her shoulders, and something else laid on her hair, soft and smooth like a little, lean, brown cheek. The memory was so pleasant that Aunt Olivia closed her eyes to make it stay. When she opened them some one was coming along the path, but it was not Rebecca Mary.

"Good afternoon!" some one said. Aunt Olivia stiffened into a Plummer again with hurried embarrassment. She did not recognize the voice nor the pleasant young face that followed it through the vines.

"It's Rebecca Mary's aunt, isn't it?" The stranger smiled. "I should know it by the family resemblance."

"We're both Plummers," Aunt Olivia answered, gravely. "Won't you come up on the porch and take a seat?"

"No, I'll sit down here on the steps - I'd rather. I think I'll sit on the lowest step for I've come on a very humble errand! I'm Rebecca Mary's teacher."

"Oh!" It was all Aunt Olivia could manage, for a sudden horror had come upon her. She had a distinct remembrance of being at the Tony Trumbullses when the school teacher came to call.

"It's - it's rather hard to say it." The young person on the lowest step laughed nervously. "I'd a good deal rather not. But I think so much of Rebecca Mary - "

The horror grew in Aunt Olivia's soul. It was something terribly like that the Tony Trumbullses' teacher had said. And like this:

"It hurts - there! But I made up my mind it was my duty to come up here and say it, and so I've come. I'm sorry to have to say - "

"Don't!" ejaculated Aunt Olivia, trembling on her Plummer pedestal. For she was laboring with the impulse to refuse to listen to this intruder, to drive her away - to say: "I won't believe a word you say! You may as well go home."

"Hoity-toity!" breathed Duty in her ear. It saved her.

"Well?" she said, gently. "Go on."

"I'm sorry to say I can't teach Rebecca Mary any more, Miss Plummer. That's what I came to tell you - "

This was awful - awful! But hot rebellion rose in Aunt Olivia's heart. There was some mistake - it was some other Rebecca Mary this person meant. She would never believe it was HERS - the Plummer one!

"Because I've taught her all I know. There! Do you wonder I chose the lowest step to sit on? But it's the truth, honest," the little teacher laughed girlishly, but there were shame spots on her cheeks - "Rebecca Mary is the smartest scholar I've got, and I've taught her all I know." In her voice there was confession to having taught Rebecca Mary a little more than that. The shame spots flickered in a halo of humble honesty.

"She's been from Percentage through the arithmetic four times - Rebecca Mary's splendid in arithmetic. And she knows the geography and grammar by heart."

Annie Hamilton Donnell

The look on Aunt Olivia's face! The transition from horror to pride was overwhelming, transfiguring.

"Rebecca Mary's smart," added the honest one on the doorstep. "*I* think she ought to have a chance. There! That's all I came for, so I'll be going. Only, I don't suppose - you don't think you'll have to tell Rebecca Mary, do you? About - about me, I mean?"

"No, I don't," Aunt Olivia assured her, warmly. Her thin, lined hand met and held for a moment the small, plump one - long enough to say, "You're a good girl - I like you," in its own way. The little teacher went away in some sort comforted for having taught Rebecca Mary all she knew. She even hummed a relieved little tune on her way home, because of the pleasant tingle in the hand that Rebecca Mary's aunt had squeezed. After all, no matter how much you dreaded doing it, it was better to tell the truth.

Aunt Olivia hummed no relieved little tune. The pride in her heart battled with the Dread there and went down. Aunt Olivia did not call the Dread by any other name. It was Duty who dared.

Confronting Aunt Olivia: "I suppose you know what it means? I suppose you know it means you've got to give Rebecca Mary a chance? When are you going to send her away to school?"

"Oh - don't!" pleaded Aunt Olivia. "You don't give me any time. There's no need of hurry - "

"I'm still a Plummer, if you're not," broke in Duty, with ironic sharpness. "The Plummers were never afraid to look their duty in the face."

"I'm - I'm looking at you," groaned Aunt Olivia, climbing painfully back on to her pedestal. "Go ahead and say it. I'm ready - only I guess you've forgot how long I've had Rebecca Mary. When you've brought a child up - "

"I brought her up myself," calmly. "I ought to know. She wouldn't have been Rebecca Mary, would she, if I hadn't been right on hand? Who was it taught her to sew patchwork before she was four years old? And make sheets - and beds - and bread? Who was it kept her from being a little tomboy like the minister's girl? Who taught her to walk instead of run, and eat with her fork, and be a lady? Who was it - "

"Oh, you - you!" sighed Aunt Olivia, trembling for her balance. "You did 'em all. I never could've alone."

"Then" - Duty was justly complacent - "Then perhaps you'll be willing to leave Rebecca Mary's going away to school to me. She must go at once, as soon as you can get her read - "

Aunt Olivia tumbled off. She did not wait to pick herself up before she turned upon this Duty that delighted in torturing her.

"You better get her ready yourself! You better let her down and make her some nightgowns and count her pocket-handkerchiefs! You think you can do anything - no, I'M talking now! I guess it's my turn. I guess I've waited long enough. Maybe you brought Rebecca Mary up, but I'm not going to leave it to you whether she'd ought to go away to school. She's my Rebecca Mary, isn't she? Well? It's me that loves her, isn't it - not you? If I can't love her and stay a Plummer, then

I'll - love her. I'm going to leave it to the minister."

The minister was a little embarrassed. The wistful look in Aunt Olivia's eyes said, "Say no" so plainly. And he knew he must say yes - the minister's Duty was imperative, too.

"If she can't get any more good out of the school here - " he began.

"She can't," said Aunt Olivia's Duty for her. "The teacher says she can't. Rebecca Mary's smart." Then Duty, too, was proud of Rebecca Mary!

"I know she is," said the minister, heartily. "My Rhoda - you ought to hear my Rhoda set her up. She thinks Rebecca Mary knows more than the teacher does."

"Rhoda's smart, too," breathed Duty in Aunt Olivia's ear.

"So you see, dear Miss Olivia, the child would make good use of any advantage - "

"You mean I ought to send her away? Well, I'm ready to - I said I'd leave it to you. Where shall I send her? If there was only - I don't suppose there's some place near to? Children go home Friday nights sometimes, don't they?"

"There is no school near enough for that, I'm afraid," the minister said, gently. He could not bear the look in Miss Olivia's eyes.

"It hurt," he told his wife afterwards. "I wish she hadn't asked me, Felicia."

"I know, dear, but it's the penalty of being a minister. Ministers' hearts ought to be coated with - with asbestos or something, so the looks in people's eyes wouldn't burn through. I'm glad she didn't ask ME!"

"It will nearly kill them both," ran on the minister's thoughts, aloud. "You know how it was when Miss Olivia was at the hospital."

"Robert!" - the minister's wife's tone was reproachful - " you're talking in the future tense! You said 'will.' Then you advised her to send Rebecca Mary away!"

"Guilty," pleaded the minister. "What else could I do?"

"You could have offered to teach her yourself" - with prompt inspiration. "Oh, Robert, why didn't you?"

"Felicia! - my dear!" - for the minister was modest.

"You know plenty for two Rebecca Marys," she triumphed. "Didn't you appropriate all the honors at college, you selfish boy!"

"It's too late now, dear." But the minister's eyes thanked her, and the big clasp of his arms. A minister may be mortal.

"Maybe it is and maybe it isn't," spoke the minister's wife, in riddles. "We'll wait and see."

"But, Felicia - but, dear, they're both them Plummers."

"Maybe they are and maybe they aren't," laughed she.

That night Aunt Olivia told Rebecca Mary - after she

went to bed, quite calmly:

"Rebecca Mary, how would you like to go away to school? For I'm going to send you, my dear."

"'Away - to school - my dear!'" echoed Rebecca Mary, sitting upright in bed. Her slight figure stretched up rigid and preternaturally tall in the dim light.

"Yes; the minister advises it - I left it to him. He thinks you ought to have advantages." Aunt Olivia slipped down suddenly beside the little rigid figure and touched it rather timidly. She felt a little in awe of the Rebecca Mary who knew more than her teacher did.

"They all seem to think you're - smart, my dear," Aunt Olivia said, and she would scarcely have believed it could be so hard to say it. For the life of her she could not keep the pride from pricking through her tone. The wild temptation to sell her Plummer birthright for a kiss assailed her. But she groped in the dimness for Duty's cool touch and found it. In the Plummer code of laws it was writ, "Thou shalt not kiss."

"I'm going right to work to make you some new nightgowns," Aunt Olivia added, hastily. "I think I shall make them plain," for it was in the nature of a reinforcement to her courage to leave off the ruffles.

Rebecca Mary's eyes shone like stars in the dark little room. The child thought she was glad to be going away to school.

"Shall I study algebra and Latin?" she demanded.

"I suppose so - that'll be what you go for."

"And French - not FRENCH?"

"Likely."

Rebecca Mary fell back on the pillows to grasp it. But she was presently up again.

"And that thing that tells about the air and - and gassy things? And the one that tells about your bones?"

Aunt Olivia did not recognize chemistry, but she knew bones. She sighed gently.

"Oh yes; I suppose you'll find out just how you're put together, and likely it'll scare you so you won't ever dare to breathe deep again. Maybe learning like that is important - I suppose the minister knows."

"The minister knows everything," Rebecca Mary said, solemnly. "If you let me go away to school, I'll try to learn to know as much as he does, Aunt Olivia. You don't - you don't think he'd mind, do you?"

In the dark Aunt Olivia smiled. The small person there on the pillows was, after all, a child. Rebecca Mary had not grown up, after all!

"He won't mind," promised Aunt Olivia for the minister. She went away presently and cut out Rebecca Mary's new nightgowns. She sat and stitched them, far into the night, and stitched her sad little bodings in, one by one. Already desolation gripped Aunt Olivia's heart.

Rebecca Mary's dreams that night were marvelous ones. She dreamed she saw herself in a glass after she had learned all the things there were to learn, and she looked like the minister! When she spoke, her voice sounded deep and sweet like the minister's voice. Somewhere a voice like the minister's wife's seemed to be calling "Robert! Robert!"

"Yes?" answered Rebecca Mary, and woke up.

There were many preparations to make. The days sped by busily, and to Rebecca Mary full of joyous expectancy. Aunt Olivia made no moan. She worked steadily over the plain little outfit and thrust her Dreads away with resolute courage, to wait until Rebecca Mary was gone. Time enough then.

"You're doing right - that ought to comfort you," encouraged Duty, kindly.

"Clear out!" was what Aunt Olivia cried out, sharply, in answer. "You've done enough - this is all your work! Don't stand there hugging yourself. YOU'RE not going to miss Rebecca Mary - "

"I shall miss her," Duty murmured. "I was awake all night, too, dreading it. You didn't know, but I was there."

The last day, when it came, seemed a little - a good deal - like that other day when Aunt Olivia went away, only it was the other way about this time. Rebecca Mary was going away on this day. The things packed snugly in the big valise were her things; it was she, Rebecca Mary, who would unpack them in a wondrous, strange place. It was Rebecca Mary the minister's wife and Rhoda came to bid good-bye.

Aunt Olivia went to the station in the stage with the child. She did not speak much on the way, but sat firmly straight and smiled. Duty had told her the last thing to smile. But Duty had not trusted her; unseen and uninvited, Duty had slipped into the jolting old vehicle between Aunt Olivia and Rebecca Mary.

"She isn't the Plummer she was once," sighed Duty.

But at the little station, in those few final moments, two Plummers, an old one and a young one, waited quietly together. Neither of them broke down nor made ado. Duty retired in palpable chagrin.

"Good-bye, my dear," Aunt Olivia said, steadily, though her lips were white.

"Good-bye, Aunt Olivia," Rebecca Mary Plummer said, steadily. "I'm very MUCH obliged to you for sending me."

"You're - welcome. Don't forget to wear your rubbers. I put in some liniment in case you need it - don't get any in your eyes."

Outside on the platform Aunt Olivia sought and found Rebecca Mary's window and stood beside it till the train started. Through the dusty pane their faces looked oddly unfamiliar to each other, and the two pairs of eyes that gazed out and in had a startled wistfulness in them that no Plummer eyes should have. If Duty had staid -

The train shook itself, gave a jerk or two, and plunged down the shining rails. Aunt Olivia watched it out of sight, then turned patiently to meet her loneliness. The

Dreads came flocking back to her as if she had beckoned to them. For now was the time.

The letters Rebecca Mary wrote were formally correct and brief. There was no homesickness in them. It was pleasant at the school, that book about bones was going to be very interesting. Aunt Olivia was not to worry about the rubbers, and Rebecca Mary would never forget to air her clothes when they came from the wash. Yes, she had aired the nightgown that Aunt Olivia ironed the last thing. No, she hadn't needed any liniment yet, but she wouldn't get any in her eyes.

Aunt Olivia's letters were to the point and calm, as though Duty stood peering over her shoulder as she wrote. She was glad Rebecca Mary liked the bones, but she was a little surprised. She was glad about the rubbers and the wash; she was glad there had been no need yet for the liniment. It was a good thing to rub on a sore throat. The minister's wife had been over with her work she said Rhoda missed Rebecca Mary. Yes, the little, white cat was well - no, she hadn't caught any mice. The calla lily had two buds, the Northern Spy tree was not going to bear very well.

"Robert, I've been to see Miss Olivia," the minister's wife said at tea.

"Yes?" The minister waited. He knew it was coming.

"She was knitting stockings for Rebecca Mary. Robert, she sat there and smiled till I had to come home to cry!"

"My dear! - do you want me to cry, too?"

"I'm a-going to," sniffed Rhoda. "I feel it coming."

"She is so lonely, Robert! It would break your heart to see her smile. How do I know she is? Oh no - no, she didn't say she was! But I saw her eyes and she let the little, white cat get up in her lap!"

"Proof enough," the minister said, gently.

Between the two of them - the child at school and Aunt Olivia at home - letters came and went for six weeks. Aunt Olivia wrote six, Rebecca Mary six. All the letters were terse and brief and unemotional. Weather, bones, little white cats, liniment - everything in them but loneliness or love. Rebecca Mary began all hers "Dear Aunt Olivia," and ended them all "Respectfully your niece, Rebecca Mary Plummer."

"Dear Rebecca Mary," began Aunt Olivia's. "Your aff. aunt, Olivia Plummer," they closed. Yet both their hearts were breaking. Some hearts break quicker than others; Plummer hearts hold out splendidly, but in the end -

In the end Aunt Olivia went to see the minister and was closeted with him for a little. The minister's wife could hear them talking - mostly the minister - but she could not hear what they said.

"It's come," she nodded, sagely. "I was sure it would. That's what the little, white cat purred when she rubbed against my skirts, 'She can't stand it much longer. She doesn't sleep nights nor eat days - she's giving out.' Poor Miss Olivia! - but I can't understand Rebecca Mary."

"It's the Plummer in her," the little, white cat would have purred. "You wait!"

Aunt Olivia turned back at the minister's study door. "Then you will?" she said, eagerly. "You're perfectly willing to? I don't want to feel - "

"You needn't feel," the minister smiled. "I'm more than willing. I'm delighted. But in the matter of - er - remuneration, I cannot let you - "

"You needn't let me," smiled Miss Olivia; "I'll do it without." She was gently radiant. Her pitifully thin face, so transfigured, touched the big heart of the minister. He went to his window and watched the slight figure hurry away. He would scarcely have been surprised to see it turn down the road that led towards the railway station.

"Oh, Robert!" It was the minister's wife at his elbow. "You dear boy, I know you've promised! You needn't tell me a thing - didn't I suggest it in the first place? Dear Miss Olivia - I'm so glad, Robert! So are you glad, you minister!" But they were neither of them thinking of little, stubbed-out shoes that would be easier to buy.

Aunt Olivia turned down the station road the next morning, in the swaying old stage. Her eager gaze never left the plodding horses, as if by looking at them she could make them go faster.

"They're pretty slow, aren't they?" she said.

"Slow - THEM? Well, I guess you weren't never a stage horse!" chuckled the old man at the reins.

"No," admitted Aunt Olivia, "I never was, but I know I'd go faster today."

At the Junction, halfway to Rebecca Mary, she descended alertly from the train and crossed the platform. She must wait here, they told her, an hour and twenty minutes. On the other side of the station a train was just slowing up, and she stood a moment to scan idly the thin stream of people that trickled from the cars. There were old women - did any of them, she wondered, feel as happy as she did? There were tall children, too. There was one - Aunt Olivia started a little and fumbled in her soft hair, under the roses in her bonnet brim, for her glasses. There was one tall child - she was coming this way - she was coming fast - she was running! Her arms were out -

"Aunt Olivia! Aunt Olivia!" the Tall Child was crying out, joyously, "Oh, Aunt Olivia!"

"Rebecca Mary! - my dear, my dear!"

They were in each other's arms. The roses on Aunt Olivia's bonnet brim slipped to one side - the two of them, not Plummers any more, but a common, glad old woman and a common, glad, tall child, were kissing each other as though they would never stop. The stream of people reached them and flowed by on either side. Trains came and went, and still they stood like that.

"Hoity-toity!" muttered Aunt Olivia's Duty, and slipped past with the stream. A Plummer to the end, what use to stay any longer there?

"I was coming home," cried Rebecca Mary. "I couldn't

bear it another minute!"

"I was coming after you - my dear, my DEAR, *I* couldn't bear it another minute!"